I0556645

The Alexis Stanton Chronicles
by
J.C. Phelps

Color Me Grey
Shades of Grey
Reflections of Grey
Traces of Grey
Fragments of Grey
Edge of Grey

J.C. PHELPS

TRACES OF GREY

THE ALEXIS STANTON CHRONICLES, BOOK 4

PUBLISHED BY
J.C. Phelps
Traces of Grey
Copyright © 2013 -2017 by J.C. Phelps

Cover design and formatting by Terry Roy

ISBN-10: 0981769047
ISBN-13: 978-0981769042

NewPub Binding, USA

Contents

Written for

Alexandra
Edy
Ellie
Jim
Rick
Robert
&
Robert

Special thanks to

Angela – Bobbe – Carmen – Dawn
Deb – Jen – Jessica – Jimmy – Karen
Linda – Lynn – Mac – Natasha
Robert – Sandy – Terry

Thank you to all of my beta readers. Without you I wouldn't have had to courage to press that publish button.

An extra big thank you to my bestest ex-Ranger friend —you know who you are and your name may or may not be listed. I'll never tell!

I'd like to express an extra hearty thank you to Mac. THANK YOU!

Chapter One

I WAS FEELING CLAUSTROPHOBIC, TRAPPED, AND restless. "You've been back in the office for a month now." I heard the whine in my voice and tried to disguise it. "When are you going to put me back to work?"

Less than two weeks ago it would have taken all of my partners to pry me away from White's side. But now he was recovered enough to be back at work. I should be back out there, too.

It had been more than two months since Ruben shot him. That was a defining moment in my life. James Ruben had learned the identity of Penumbra so my father had locked him up to protect my mother. Colin had unwittingly let him out in hopes he would lead them to the mob boss,

Dimitri Glasgov. Instead, Ruben went straight to my mother to kill her. He wanted to get even with my father for locking him up.

Something clicked inside as I watched White fall to the floor that night. The agony I felt in that short moment had the potential to bring me to my knees. As he fell in slow motion I had a moment of clarity. I knew I would be lost without him. As my knees threatened to buckle my training kicked in and I instinctively took care of the threat. Karma is a bitch when you're a bad guy, and Ruben quickly found out that I'd recently changed my name to Karma. I fired my weapon. I was only slightly disgruntled that Ruben probably didn't even have time to realize what happened before he was lying dead in a pool of blood on my parent's floor.

The memory of White falling to the floor was something I'd carry forever. It made me sick to my stomach every time I let it play through. I'd gotten better at repressing the memory by having White constantly at my side.

"You are working." White's voice pulled me out of the nightmare.

"No, I'm not. I'm hanging out and watching you and Gabriella work. I need to get back out there. The only excitement I've had in months is that Angel Moran concert Gabriella took me to."

Angel was one of my favorite artists at the moment, but it was sad that I'd even compare a few hours at a concert to what had become my life. Still, it was all I had.

"Maybe you could put me through some more training if you aren't going to put me on a job." I begged. "Has anything come down the pipes for Penumbra?"

"No. Just the one you passed on when I was still recovering. Penumbra might be the most sought after assassin in the world, but he's too expensive or exclusive for just anyone. You should go back and figure out how many hits he did before the switch. That might give you a better idea of how often you can expect to get one of those jobs."

"I suppose. I just thought I'd be busier now." I sighed and slumped a little more in my chair.

"Okay. I do have plans for you. I just wasn't ready to put you back out there yet."

My spirits brightened. "Really? What is it? When?"

His smile had a hint of sensuality that made my insides burn. A memory that I savored regularly was the kiss we'd shared just before he'd been shot and the look he gave me brought me right back to that spot. I regretted that it had never gone any further. While caring for him in those first few weeks, I assumed we were a couple because of that kiss. It felt like I'd signed a contract with that kiss, an unbreakable contract. As he grew stronger and his fire returned, I expected us to continue where we left off. The tension was still there, so I knew the attraction was there too, but his lack of ambition, when it came to follow through, threatened to push me over the edge.

Too many times to count we'd brushed past one another. We'd linger but not long enough to allow the heat to build.

One of us always backed off. I'd come to accept that this was to be our relationship and was determined to be okay with it.

"That's why you fit right in. You're always ready to take on the next job." His face turned grim, but it didn't last before he put his boss face on. "Actually, I have a couple of options for you. You need some isolation training, flight training, and then there's EOD but—"

Again, the less than pleased look flashed across his face. It only replaced his cocky half grin for less than a length of a blink, but I noticed it and it shook my own confidence.

I waited with my stomach in my throat.

"I'd hoped to keep you here for a bit longer. You're going to be gone for months at a time for this training."

I swallowed hard. Did he just admit he didn't want me to leave? Though I'd convinced myself that I was okay with a flirt buddy, I still hoped. Now he was telling me this. He didn't want me gone for months? My heart leaped, but I quickly got it under control. The last thing I wanted was to relive that moment when I realized we'd never take it further. I couldn't allow the hope to rise above the disappointment. I didn't know how well I'd cope. I took a deep breath and was about to ask how long each training option would take when the phone rang. I remained quiet as we waited for Gabriella's voice over the intercom.

"Mr. White?" Her voice broke the silence as expected.

"Yes?" he answered as he pushed the button.

"Admiral Stanton. Line one."

"Thank you, Gabriella." White gave me a shoulder shrug and a hike of the eyebrows for an apology as he lifted the receiver to his ear.

I studied my hands as he spoke with the Admiral. Maybe he'd have a quick job for me, but chances were the job wouldn't be big enough to send me out. The Admiral had a budget, even if it didn't seem like it at times.

The conversation was quick and ended with White saying, "I'll get someone right on it, Admiral."

White replaced the receiver. "The Admiral wants me to put a man on an intel-gathering mission."

I nodded and expected him to start making calls to set it up but instead he narrowed his eyes at me. I could almost see the wheels turning and wondered what he was up to.

"What?" My temperature rose. Prolonged eye contact with White always made my blood boil.

His smile became calculating. "We could do this one together. We'd just have to take a pay cut. The Admiral said he didn't want to pay much for this one." He shrugged.

"What are the details?"

White explained the target was expected to be in Jamaica next week, and the objective was to take pictures of him and all of his security detail.

"Why?"

"I have no idea and I really don't care. Your father has his reasons, and that's good enough for me."

"I guess you're right. We don't have to shoot him with anything but a camera. I don't really care, either."

"Interested?" He asked.

"Jamaica?"

"Jamaica," he repeated with a slight eyebrow hike.

I took a deep breath. The two of us in Jamaica, away from everyone else, with an easy job and probably extra time scared the shit out of me, and so did the gleam in his eyes. He had that *I have a plan that can't fail* sparkle. He seemed determined to make the hope rise to the top.

His confidence and aggressive posture reassured me when I was about to do a job with him, but this time I was the target. White was deadly and maybe he'd just been easy on me so far. As soon as I felt any signs of dismay in our flirts I'd back away but there had been times I'd decided to go through with it, and he still backed off. I have to stop the hope from building. I guess the fear on my face wasn't a big turn on. Maybe that was why he backed off.

His animalistic expressions always made me work to remain in control, and I could tell by the glint in his eyes he was going to do everything in his power to make me relinquish that control. Honestly, I wanted to give in but feared it would screw everything up. Our working relationship was important, but I was terrified I wouldn't be good enough for him. He was experienced, and I was anything but. I'd never been with a man before. Anthony didn't count and not just because I didn't remember it.

I swallowed hard. My tension must have shown on my face because White's attitude changed again. His inner beast sank deeper, softening his face. I'd seen this look before, too. It brought up even stronger emotions than his lecherous guise. It made me feel confident and secure, warm and comfortable inside a fog of amour. Or was it just desire? The hope had risen slightly above the acceptable line. I knew he was about to cave and scrap his plan and I couldn't let him. Not this time.

"When do we leave then?" I decided not to think this one through because I knew I'd find a reason not to do it. Somewhere inside that warm, enveloping fog the fact that this was a job first made it easier. Even if I ended up being disappointed I could always blame it on the job.

"I'll have to make travel arrangements and find us a place to stay," he said. "Let me work it through and I'll let you know later."

I took a deep breath and stood. "Can you email me the info so I can do a little research on the target before we go?"

"Right away."

We'd both reverted to work mode and the fog of sexual tension mixed with the want to be loved dissipated.

"I'll call you with our departure time as soon as I get it set up," he called out as I crossed the threshold between his office and Gabriella's.

"Sounds good." I shut his door.

I knew Gabriella was watching me exit White's office. She watched almost everyone exit. But, for some reason, I felt like I shouldn't make eye contact with her, as if I'd just done something wrong.

"Can you say where you're going?" Gabriella looked up from her computer screen. The smile that occupied her face disappeared. "Is everything okay?" Her brow furrowed and she placed both of her hands flat on her desk, preparing to stand.

"Yes. Why?"

"You look ill, sweetie. What's going on?" She hadn't relaxed her stance and if I didn't explain, she'd be at my side consoling me for whatever she thought might be wrong.

"Nothing's wrong. We are going to Jamaica. Intel-gathering for the Admiral."

"Jamaica! You are so lucky, girl." She relaxed and sat back into her chair with a sly look. "White's going." This wasn't a question. "It'll be just the two of you then?"

"Yep."

Gabriella knew my feelings and knew that nothing had happened yet.

"No wonder you look sick." Her grin broadened. "Don't forget there is nothing wrong with combining business with pleasure. Find your strength and make the first move."

She winked and I smiled back at her.

"Shhhh." I pointed at White's closed door. "I have no idea what to pack." I couldn't talk about this in the front office.

"Your bikini. That's it. You don't need anything else. Unless you have more than one."

"I'll figure it out." I laughed. "We'll be leaving as soon as White makes the arrangements, so I've got to go."

"If I don't see you for a while, have a great time and stay safe. Oh! Don't forget sunscreen. That stuff comes in handy for lots of things." Her eyebrows were still dancing as I shut the office door behind me.

INSTEAD OF PACKING I WENT straight to my computer and checked my email. White had already sent me the info, so I did a quick search for the target. I was rewarded with a photo and a dossier. Mateo Ruiz was a known drug dealer operating out of Ecuador with connections across the globe. Though I'd told White I didn't care why I was doing this, I couldn't help but wonder what was going to come down on this man. The Admiral asking for information about his security detail indicated that they planned to breach that security somehow, and soon.

I shook Ruiz out of my mind and looked up the resort. It was very elite and very private. If White got us in I'd be impressed. The layout was simple, and included its very own private beach.

For being so elite and private, their computers weren't well protected, and I'd pulled up their reservation records within seconds. Mr. Ruiz was scheduled in a six-bedroom villa right on the beach. Very private and easily defended from everything but prying eyes.

The ringing of my phone made me jerk in my chair.

"HELLO?"

"The resort is booked and I can't get us in," White's voice gave me goose bumps when it was so close to my ear.

"I wondered. So, what's the plan?"

"I just got off the phone with Gary Waterstone and he's agreed to take us out on his yacht."

"Waterstone?"

"He's an old friend of the family and he's a steady client for the company." He continued to explain. "Waterstone caters to high profile clients, so we keep a couple of men on his yacht. I'd ask them to do it, but—" I could hear a smile in his voice. "I really want to get out on that yacht and Waterstone would rather I not pull our guys off their security detail."

"Security on a charter yacht?"

"He caters to high profile clients."

"Like who?"

"Like us." He said this as if we might actually need a security detail.

I almost laughed.

"It'll be fun." White continued. "I've always wanted to go out on his yacht. It's amazing but expensive."

"Will the Admiral pick up the expense?"

"No. He specifically said *no one special on this one.* That means he doesn't want to pay a lot for the info."

"How do we justify it?"

"I gave Waterstone a discount on his security detail for the next six months. The Admiral will pick up some of the expense, it'll work itself out."

"When will we leave?" My excitement and my fear were at equal levels.

"We can leave as soon as I track Brown down. We'll need him to fly us out to the yacht. Waterstone is already on his way to Jamaica on a charter. Thankfully, there's just enough room for us on the yacht."

"We are going all out for this low paying gig."

"It's okay. It'll work out. Did you figure out a plan of attack?"

"Not yet. I think, if we can get the boat to anchor off shore in front of the resort, we might be able to get the photos we need. Depending on Ruiz's routine, we may need to go ashore. I'm emailing you the ideal area on the water to get pictures of him at the resort."

"Sounds good. I'm sure I can get Waterstone to anchor where I need him to. Get packed because we'll be leaving as soon as I can track down Brown. Oh," he added before he hung up, "I'll take care of the equipment. You just worry about yourself."

Chapter Two

I WAS STILL PACKING WHEN I heard Brown's knock rattle my door. I stopped what I was doing and hurried to let him in.

"You ready?" He was surly and ruffled.

"Not yet. What's wrong?" I pointed at him, indicating his appearance.

"I was *busy*," he said with a huff.

"Doing what? Sleeping?" I asked while I tried to straighten his hair.

"I wasn't sleeping, but I was in bed." He was mightily pleased with this statement, so I smacked him alongside his head messing up my previous efforts.

"Ewww!"

He laughed and pushed his way into my apartment. "I'll help you haul your stuff to the chopper."

"No. I don't want you touching any of my stuff. Gross!"

Again, he laughed and took a seat at my kitchen bar. "Hurry up."

I did as I was told and the two of us were on the roof climbing into the chopper within ten minutes.

White was already in his seat. "Took you long enough," he directed at Brown.

"Get over it. I didn't finish the project I was working on because you called. Be happy I'm here." Brown's surly attitude returned and I kept my mouth shut.

"What project?" White asked.

"Please." I held up my hands. "Please don't ask. I do not want to hear anything about it."

Brown's grin returned and White caught on. "Sorry, man." He'd adopted his own grin and I scowled.

Brown flew us to the local airport and we transferred to a small jet.

"Why didn't we just drive to the airport?"

"Traffic sucks," White replied as we loaded our gear and bags onto the jet.

"Wait until you see this yacht," Brown cut in. "You'll understand the hurry." He looked at White. "Are you sure there isn't room for one more on this one?"

"Positive. Maybe next time."

"I'd love to take a pay cut for a few months to run with Waterstone. I'm qualified." Brown said.

"You'd go back to security just to waste your time away on that yacht?"

"For a few months. Hell yeah."

The two men continued to chat as they entered the cockpit and I was left in the cabin alone. I took a seat near the back of the cabin because they faced toward the front of the plane and I could see both White and Brown as well as get a slight view out the windshield.

I could clearly hear the men talking, but I didn't pay much attention until I heard White ask Brown if this new woman was a keeper.

"I doubt it. But, she's fun *and* famous so I'll hang in as long as I can."

"Famous? Who?"

"I'm sure I'll tell you someday, but since you want to know, I'll keep it to myself."

"Ah. Of course. Let me know when you've figured out who you wish you were dating."

"You won't believe me unless I walk up to you with her on my arm so we'll leave it at that."

"Fair enough. I promise I won't believe you until you prove it to me."

The men laughed and my thoughts drifted again. Every once in a while, one of the men turned in their seat to include me in their conversation, but I was so distracted by the thought of being practically alone with White in a romantic environment that I wasn't worth talking to. By the time White came back to check on me I was feeling sick to my stomach, and my skin was clammy. If I had to make the first move I'd probably just throw up on him.

"Are you okay? You aren't getting motion sickness are you?" He reached out for my forehead.

"No. I'm fine." I moved the loose strands of hair from my face before he could.

He narrowed his eyes.

"I'm serious. I'm fine."

"Okay, then." He turned his back on me.

"How much longer?" I asked as he maneuvered back into the co-pilot's chair.

"We'll land in less than ten minutes," Brown threw back over his shoulder. "Are you sure you're feeling okay? You still have a short chopper ride. I'd be happy to fill in for you." He'd turned away from me, but not before I caught the broad grin.

"I'm fine, Brown. Don't you want to get back to your mysterious lady friend?"

"I wouldn't mind, but I'd rather go for a cruise on that yacht."

Shortly after that we were on the ground and collecting our bags.

"Let me know when you need a ride home," Brown called after us as we exited the plane.

"Brown's not flying us the rest of the way?" I asked when he didn't get out of the plane with us.

"No. Gary's sending someone to get us."

We made our way to another part of the airport and were greeted by a familiar face.

"Commanders." Sam stood at attention. He was clean-shaven with a tight haircut and a pilot's uniform. When I first met Sam he'd picked White and me up in Fairbanks to fly us to the Alaskan compound. He was my main pick from that compound for my elite team, Team Grey. Realizing I'd been designated the head of the elite team always gave me a rush of pride. Why was he here? He should be off doing elite team stuff or training troops.

"I wish you wouldn't salute, Sam. We're here on a job, but I'd rather everyone didn't know that."

Sam smiled and stuck out his hand instead. White grabbed it in a familiar grip and they pulled each other into a hug. Some of my partners made it clear they didn't like to be saluted, but I suspected Brown and Red reveled in it.

"Good to see you again, *Ms.* Grey." Sam avoided tacking on the commander title. It always made me uncomfortable anyway. I didn't really earn that title but had been given it by default. He held out his hand to me as soon as he and White were clear of one another. I was pulled into a similarly rough embrace.

"You look good in that uniform, Sam. Being a part of Team Grey has its perks." I tugged on his lapel as we separated.

"Thank you, ma'am. Yes, it does." He held his head a little higher.

"So, how's the job?" White asked as Sam led the way to his chopper.

"Good. I'm getting tired of all the luxury, though. It's not easy, you know."

They laughed.

"I am going to have to switch you out before long." White said. "It'll be time to train a new batch of recruits, and I really need your help."

"I know it. I need to get back out there. I can feel myself getting softer every day. I wasn't completely kidding about this not being easy. The yacht has an exercise room, but it's hard to utilize when I'm on duty all the time."

"You can't be flying all the time," I said.

"No, but I do have other duties, and then there's the view. It's quite distracting. And it doesn't help that I haven't eaten better in my entire life."

"Did Gary say anything to you about why we're here?" White asked.

"He only informed me that you are allowed to do whatever you want on the yacht without question. Plus, you have run of the chopper if you need it. Even said to allow you to pilot if you need to."

"I expected him to let me brief you. Glad he hasn't lost his sense of propriety." White's voice held a hint of satisfaction. "Grey and I might need a little help with a simple surveillance job. I'm hoping it'll be quick and painless."

The flight out on the chopper didn't take as long as I thought it might and I was soon staring down at a large and beautiful boat.

"Is it a boat or a ship?" I asked as we descended.

"This is *Carmen's Retreat* ." Sam answered with pride in his voice. It was almost as if the yacht belonged to him.

"As beautiful as I remember." White said.

"Isn't she?" Sam sighed.

Neither of them answered my question, so I decided I'd call *her* a boat. I knew I'd be corrected if it were considered a ship. Mariners were particular with that kind of thing, I'd found. I didn't know the size requirement for the classifications, but I knew a ship was bigger than a boat.

"Let me get those, ma'am." A young man, wearing the same uniform as Sam, took my bag and handed it off to the porter, then reached back to help me from the chopper.

"So happy to have you join us, Commander Grey. I've heard a lot about you."

"No commander talk this trip, Billy." Sam eyeballed the porter gathering our luggage. "She's just Ms. Grey at the moment."

Billy smiled. "Ms. Grey," he tried it out. "Very glad to meet you."

Poor Billy, I thought as I watched him struggling to acknowledge White. It seemed physically painful for him not to stand at attention and salute White.

"Mr. White." He finally greeted him.

"It's been a long time, Billy. How've you been?" White extended his hand. Billy hesitated but recovered and took White's hand with a firm shake.

"Good. Thank you, sir." He beamed. "Scott will show you to your suite." He indicated the older man waiting for us who wore a haughty expression that matched his crisp uniform. Scott gave a terse nod that I almost missed as the porter crossed between us to retrieve our bags.

"You go on ahead, Alex," White said. "I've got a few things I'd like to discuss with the men before I get settled."

I wondered what he was going to discuss with them, but I didn't argue. I didn't want to crush Billy's hero worship he had going on. But, as soon as I reached Scott I turned to look back at the men in hopes of catching a glimpse of the conversation. I hadn't had any real cause to use my lip reading skills lately and this could be good practice.

"Ma'am?" Scott questioned.

"One moment Scott," I held up my finger.

I squinted my eyes to watch White say something about trusting their discretion and then he looked up at me and mouthed, "Stop it."

Sam and Billy followed his gaze and I instantly felt very conspicuous.

I turned my attention back to Scott and followed him from the helipad toward my suite.

"Here we are, ma'am. If you'd like, I can give you a full tour while Mr. White speaks with the Captain," Scott said as he opened my door for me.

"That sounds great. Do I have time to change first?"

"Of course. I'll wait outside the door."

I went to my bag and realized White's bag was right next to mine as well as all of the equipment. I went straight to the door and opened it to find Scott.

"Scott. Mr. White's bag is in my room. He might want it in his."

"My apologies, Ms. Grey. This is Mr. White's room too. This was the only suite available when Mr. White requested to board and he assured me that one room would be satisfactory."

"Crap."

"Ma'am?"

"I'm sorry, Scott. I wasn't expecting this. If it's all you have, I'll have to make do. Thank you. I won't be long."

Maybe I *am* experiencing motion sickness, I thought as I shut the door and ran for the bathroom. I hovered over the toilet for a couple of minutes but managed to keep everything down. I truly didn't think I could make the first move, but if he didn't I knew I'd be ready to kill someone in a day or two. I brushed my teeth and changed into a happy little dress and put on my sandals instead of my heavy boots.

"Ready," I said as I met Scott outside in the corridor.

He smiled. "You look much more comfortable, ma'am. If you'll follow me—"

What did he mean, more comfortable? I worried I might not be fancy enough for this yacht. The decorations and layout were opulent and lavish, and I was wearing a cute, casual dress.

I caught a glimpse of some other passengers sitting at a bar. My wardrobe anxiety dropped away when I noticed they wore clothes similar to mine.

"That is Mr. and Mrs. Klingman. They take this trip every year."

"Klingman? The name sounds familiar." I squinted my eyes to get a better look at the older couple. The squinting didn't help. It just made them look a little blurry.

"It should. They're big names in Hollywood circles. Each of them inherited unspeakable sums from their families and use it to back blockbuster movies. I don't know how they choose which movies to invest in, but chances are, if you've been backed by the Klingmans you've got a hit on your hands." He stopped. "Would you care for a drink from the bar?"

"How long before we get to Jamaica?"

"About three days."

"Then I'd love one."

It might be a good idea to calm down a little before I saw White again. This sharing-a-room nonsense gave me a little thrill. But, it should have been presented to me before the trip, especially since there was only one bed and we had our own men on the ship who would eventually talk. Maybe that's what White was lecturing the guys about at the helipad.

"What would you like?"

"I don't care. Surprise me."

He nodded and I took a seat on one of the couches scattered around the deck while I waited. I was surprised that none of the passengers seemed to care that we'd been flown in. No one other than crew greeted us and I was certain they heard us coming before we landed. Choppers weren't quiet. I was out of earshot but was able to make out the plump and red-cheeked Mrs. Klingman's lips asking Scott who I was.

"Ms. Grey, ma'am."

"No first name?" Mr. Klingman asked.

"None that she has shared, sir. I can tell you that she comes from patriotic and wealthy stock." This satisfied the couple and I watched as he returned with a glass of champagne. At least they noticed, even if they *are* too good to acknowledge us personally, I thought.

"I hope this will be to your taste, ma'am."

"I'm sure it's perfect." I took a sip as he continued the tour. The champagne was sweet and bubbly. I could sit and drink the stuff until I fell over.

We slowly made our way around the berthing deck as he pointed out the dining room, the bar we'd just come from and one of the pool areas. The exercise room and a theater were also located on this deck.

"How many passengers do you have on board?"

"Now that you and Mr. White have joined us, ten."

"And you're at full capacity?"

"We can carry more passengers but the suites aren't at full capacity. We have two single men aboard who each have their own rooms. Again, I apologize. I didn't realize you would be uncomfortable with the arrangements. I wish there was something I could do to accommodate you."

"No. I'm fine. I'm just curious. Where is everyone?" I'd gotten such a warm welcome from the Klingmans I was eager to meet the rest of the passengers.

"They are probably at the other pool and Jacuzzi area." He pointed above us.

"My first name is Alex if you are questioned again," I told him as we made our way up a deck.

"Ma'am?"

"The Klingmans," I said. "You're welcome to call me Alex, too." For some reason his formality made me a little uncomfortable and I wanted him to know I wasn't as pretentious as the rest of his passengers, at least the Klingmans. Plus, he'd been appropriately discrete when being questioned. This made me feel like he was on my side.

He stopped and turned around on the steps. "It's very nice to make your acquaintance, Alex." He took my hand in his and gave it a squeeze. "However, I will probably refrain in front of the other passengers. I hope you understand."

"That's entirely up to you." We smiled at each other and he led me up the rest of the stairs. His shoulders seemed more relaxed and his expression was one of satisfaction.

The sun was split in half by the horizon. The brilliant oranges, reds, and pinks danced in the sky as well as on the water. A cool breeze tickled my bare arms, giving me goose bumps. I fought the urge to rub some warmth back into my arms. Scott had been especially accommodating and I didn't want him to think he needed to run for a jacket. I tore my eyes away from the setting sun to look into the water below us. It was a deep blue and I could see the lights around the ship starting to illuminate the water around us. I breathed in the air and sighed.

Once at the railing we stood watching the water roll by and the sun sink further into the ocean for a couple of minutes. I used this moment to assess the rest of the passengers who were scattered across the deck. Sam stood in one corner keeping an eye on things.

Two couples were relaxing in the Jacuzzi and the two single men were at the bar, ogling the bikini-clad bartender. Everyone had already noticed me but I pretended to be completely taken with the view while I questioned Scott.

"The men and women in the Jacuzzi?"

"Mr. and Mrs. Stoddard and Mr. and Mrs. Jenkins." Scott replied without missing a beat. "Mrs. Stoddard is a well known plastic surgeon and her husband—"

"Yes?"

"Is not." He looked out at the sunset with great interest.

I chuckled. "Trophy?"

"Yes, ma'am," he smiled.

"He certainly looks a bit younger than her."

"Don't tell her that and don't get caught alone with him. He's not a faithful husband and she's not a forgiving woman."

"Good to know. Mr. and Mrs. Jenkins?"

"Janet and Steve. Janet is Mrs. Stoddard's sister and this is their first time on a luxury yacht. They own a small grocery store in Canal Point Florida. Very down to earth couple with two kids in high school."

"The two men at the bar?"

"Brothers. Joel and Pete Dante. Successful internet entrepreneurs. Very single and proving it both on the ship as well as in port."

"You are perfect, Scott. Now, can you tell me where I might find Mr. White?"

"Probably still catching up with the captain."

"I imagine it wouldn't be appropriate for me to go wandering in there." I mused aloud.

"I won't stop you, ma'am," he said.

"Thank you, but I think I should probably behave this early in the trip. I do have to share a room with the man for at least three more days."

"Sound thinking, ma'am." He took my champagne flute. "May I get you another before dinner?"

"Why not? When is dinner?"

He checked his watch. "Thirty minutes. No need to dress for dinner."

I nodded and handed him my glass.

I watched the lips of the two young men as they asked Scott their questions. The Jenkins' and Stoddards had moved to the bar as soon as Scott approached. They were all listening intently at the sparse information he was doling out. Apparently, none of them knew we'd be joining them this afternoon and we were the talk of the boat. Again, he gave my name as Ms. Grey and did not give them my occupation.

I wasn't sure if he knew my occupation but I was certain he'd heard Billy call me Commander Grey so he had to have some idea. The man was obviously not dumb.

After Scott returned with my drink he told me he had other duties to attend to and left me staring out at the still sinking sun. Sam joined me at the railing.

"Beautiful, isn't it."

"Yes it is." I was thinking how I would have liked to share my first sunset on the yacht with White, even if I was mad at him for not telling me we'd have to share the suite.

"White asked me to be discrete about the two of you staying in the same cabin. He doesn't want to damage your reputation."

"If I had known we were to be in the same room I might not have come," I admitted.

"He worried that you might be upset because you didn't know and asked me to speak with you."

"Isn't he so sweet." I gave Sam a direct look. "And you too." I pinched his cheek. The champagne was beginning to work its magic. "Don't worry. Neither of you will have to keep me from making a scene."

He grinned. "It's that black eye you gave Brown back at the Nevada compound. It has me a little worried."

"Don't worry, Sam. I only pass out black eyes when Brown unexpectedly grabs my ass."

"Is that what he did?" His eyes widened. "I always wondered. He told us so many different stories I didn't know which one to believe. Figures it would be a story that was never told."

"He planned the entire thing to make the guys think I was unpredictable and mean."

"Oh no, not Brown." His voice was thick with sarcasm and his look was gleeful. "How is he, anyway?"

"He's got a new girlfriend. Says she's famous."

"Really? She probably is."

"You think?"

"Fairly certain. He never lies about women, even if it gets him razzed."

I'd heard the men talking about their past conquests and knew Brown was a hopeless romantic. It was easy to forget because he didn't go out of his way to treat me like the women in his stories. We'd become close because of his teasing, but if he'd had any interest in me, he would never treat me that way. I was just one of the guys who happened to be a woman. He'd treat the rest of our partners the same way if they had the parts. I used to think he was a pig. However, his personality and almost perpetual happy mood had grown on me, and I wouldn't trade the harassment for more respect. That was his way to show me that he thought of me as an equal who could handle my position.

"I wonder who it is?"

"I'm sure we'll all find out soon enough. If he doesn't bring her into the office he'll get pictures to prove it and I'll get an email one of these days. But, I won't get that email until they are no longer an item."

We remained at the railing for several more minutes. The deck had cleared out. Even the bartender had left her post.

"Can I escort you down to dinner, ma'am?" Sam held out his arm.

We were the last of the passengers to walk into the dining room. White stood and met us.

"Everything okay?" He asked.

"For now," I answered.

Sam left us and White escorted me to the one long table in the room. He pulled out my chair next to his and waited until I sat before taking his own.

"You look nice," he said.

The table was abuzz with private conversations. The cute bartender from upstairs actually had clothes on and was pouring wine for the guests.

We'd been seated at the right arm of the captain and White finally introduced me to Captain Waterstone.

"Gary, this is Ms. Grey. Alex, this is Gary," he nodded across the table to a beautiful brunette, "and Carmen."

I assumed she was the woman the boat was named for. She looked to be in her fifties but still carried a youthful smile that was very welcoming. She had a kind face. The captain was close to Carmen's age and his face exhibited a strong confidence.

"Nice to meet you Captain and Mrs. Waterstone." I nodded to them.

"Please, call me Gary."

"And me Carmen," the captain's wife added.

"Gary and Carmen." I smiled.

"I better do the introductions," Gary stood from his seat. The table quieted as soon as everyone noticed the captain standing.

"Good evening. I would normally let you all make your own introductions but since they boarded a little late into the cruise I'll introduce our newest passengers." He swept his arm in our direction. "This is Mr. White and Ms. Grey, good friends of mine."

I expected a little more flourish and explanation but that was all he had. He returned to his seat and the crew took that as their cue to serve dinner. The conversation resumed and Mrs. Stoddard, seated to right, asked, "Friends of the captain?"

"Yes. Nice to meet you Mrs. Stoddard." I smiled at her. Her look of shock was unmistakable and satisfying.

"You know my name?"

"Of course, ma'am."

"Sully said Billy called you Commander. Commander of what?" Her snooty face firmly back in place, she said this as if in a challenge.

Sully must be the crewmember who retrieved our bags.

"I command many things, ma'am." I accepted her challenge. "But, I'm on vacation right now. You're an amazing surgeon, I hear."

I didn't know what White wanted to tell these people and since the Captain hadn't divulged much I thought it might be best to remain tight lipped. Besides, mystery always adds to the respect level.

"I've earned the respect I'm owed." She sipped at her soup and I followed her lead. Thankfully, she'd had enough of me.

I stuck my tongue out at her in my mind and then mentally punched her in the nose while I sipped my own soup. The thoughts lightened my mood significantly and I felt a satisfied smile on my face.

The conversation around the table continued in intimate exchanges as we ate. Napkins dabbed at the corners of mouths as White leaned in close.

"How is everything?" He indicated the soup.

"Very good. What is it?"

"A chowder of some kind. This is only the first course."

I put my spoon down and turned to face him. "So, who gets the bed?" I asked quietly.

"I thought we'd share. I know how to keep my hands to myself. I've been doing it for a long time now."

"True, but the men will talk. You know they will."

"No they won't. Not Sam and definitely not Billy. Not after the conversation we had this afternoon."

"What was that conversation?"

"I told them to not read anything into us sharing a room. We are on a job and that's it."

I assumed he'd told them something like this, but I hoped he was lying to them.

"You missed a beautiful sunset."

I changed the subject because I didn't want to think about sharing a bed with White for anything other than sleep, or the more probable scenario of this being nothing but a job.

"You had good company and I didn't want to interrupt."

"Sam *is* good company," I agreed.

We made small talk through the rest of the meal and took our leave as soon as the captain retired from the table.

Once inside our room I flopped onto the bed and White rummaged through his things. He pulled out a clean shirt and took off the one he was wearing.

"Whoa." I shielded my eyes from the view but peeked through my fingers.

He laughed and tossed the unwashed shirt at me. "I'm going for a walk around the ship and possibly take a swim. Would you care to join me?" He reached into his bag and pulled out swim trunks.

"You *will* put those on in there." I stabbed my finger toward the bathroom.

Again he laughed. "I planned on it. So, are you coming?"

"Yeah, I'll come."

"Do you have your trunks on?"

"I don't wear *trunks.* "

I was already digging through my pack. There were dressers available but I hadn't transferred my things to them yet and probably wouldn't transfer anything but items I'd be willing to never see again.

"Can you stay in the bathroom until I'm dressed, please?"

He bowed and went to the bathroom and shut the door. I quickly changed into my bikini and pulled my dress back on over the top.

"Ready," I called out.

He exited the bathroom and held out his arm. "Shall we?"

The two of us made our way to the upper deck and directly to the bar. The bartender was in position and Scott stood off to the side, watching and waiting. Sam and Billy were inconspicuously placed in opposite corners but there were no passengers on deck.

"What would you like?" White asked when we took our seats.

"I don't care."

The stars were bright in the sky. It reminded me of being out at the cabin. White ordered me a shot of whiskey with a cola back and I shuddered inwardly. I wasn't in the mood for whiskey.

The bartender placed our drinks in front of us, pulling my attention away from the sky. I grimaced and White said, "I thought you said you didn't care."

"I didn't plan on getting drunk, just having a drink."

"Just do your shot and then I'll get you something else."

I did as I was told and sipped my cola. The whiskey burned as it went down. Scott moved to the bar and spoke briefly with the bartender and soon I had a glass of champagne in front of me. The burning sensation remained so I didn't immediately switch from my cola to the glass of champagne but I smiled at Scott as he moved away.

White made small talk with the bartender and found out her name was Sydney. I suspected she landed this job as much on her looks as her skill as a bartender. Her figure mimicked a top-heavy hourglass. Her boobs couldn't be real. They hardly moved and she was doing a lot of giggling. I relaxed back in my chair and pretended to not pay any attention. Why did men like women with obvious issues? I liked my own figure and didn't feel the need to enhance anything. But, the attention these women got for being fake made me question myself. I blamed Mrs. Stoddard for this inequity and pushed her right off of my *people I want to know* list.

"Are you okay to swim?" White asked as he removed his shirt. My eyes went directly to his scar but I shook the memory off.

"Yeah, I'm good." I stood and pulled off my dress.

I watched White closely as I did this to see if I had any effect on him and I wasn't disappointed. My boobs didn't compare to the cute bartender's but at least he was looking at mine now.

He allowed me to lead the way to the pool and I stepped in gingerly. I expected the water to be cold but the pool was heated and the water was warmer than the air around us.

I dove in and swam to the other side. When I came up for air I turned around and White was directly behind me, grinning.

I splashed him, "You scared me."

He splashed me back. "That was the point," he swam off toward the opposite end of the pool.

I relaxed against the side of the pool and watched his muscles working through the water. I realized I wore a broad grin when he came up out of the water in front of me.

"This is nice, isn't it?" He slicked his hair back from his face.

"It is." I jumped up and tried to dunk him but he was too quick and strong. I had my hands on his shoulders pushing for everything I was worth and he didn't budge. Finally, he went under but grabbed me at the knees when he came back up. Within seconds, he dumping me face first into the water.

I came up sputtering and splashed him again. We grinned openly and I took off for the opposite side of the pool. I could hear him behind me but he wasn't gaining. I reached the wall and jumped out before he made it to me. As soon as he reached the wall I dove in past him and swam another lap with him right behind me.

"Wanna race?" I asked when he took his place on the wall next to me.

"Two laps?"

"Two? Big wimp. How about ten?"

"You're on." He pushed off from the wall and I was right behind him and stayed behind him until the last lap when he fell back. I wondered what he was up to because he'd just stopped in the middle of the pool until I passed him and then he picked up his swimming right behind me. When I was about to grab the wall and win the race I knew his plan.

He yanked my leg and pulled me behind him. I surfaced and splashed him again.

"Jerk." Then I noticed more voices all around us. The deck had filled. I looked around and most of them had their suits on but must have held back from entering the pool because of our race.

White had already exited the pool and held his hand down to help me out. I took it and he lifted me out of the pool as if I weighed nothing. Scott, already poolside, handed us towels. I immediately started to dry my face. The conversations around the pool stopped for a moment. I had a horrible vision of me standing there, just me, and my bikini floating in the water. I quickly made sure I was still dressed and felt better when I heard splashes.

I made my way back to the bar and my waiting glass of champagne. One of the Dante boys was already comfortable in the seat next to mine.

"You're a good swimmer," he said.

"Joel, right?" I asked.

"Yes, and that's my brother, Pete." He pointed to his brother about to dive into the pool.

"Alex." I held out my hand.

He took it and instead of the shake I expected he turned my hand over and kissed it.

White's hand stretched across my shoulder toward Joel. "Nice to meet you, Joel. You can call me White."

Joel took White's hand and I could tell White squeezed a little harder than he needed to.

"So." Joel's voice had gone up an octave but he cleared his throat and continued. "What is it you do?" He now directed all his attention toward White.

"Ms. Grey and I are partners in a private military corporation. We provide the security here on the ship," he answered.

"Really? So Sam and Billy really work for you?"

"Yep."

"That's why they called you commander. But, you?" He gave me a shocked look.

I raised my eyebrows and took in a deep breath. I heard White snickering behind me and I shot him a dirty look.

"Ms. Grey can hold her own, Joel. Trust me."

I downed my champagne and asked Sydney for a refill.

"Private Military?" Mr. Klingman's voice joined the conversation.

"Yes, George, a PMC. White and Associates to be exact." White had gotten better info than I did because he knew everyone's first name.

"What exactly do you do?" Mrs. Klingman asked.

"We do a lot of different things."

I piped up and gave the explanation that Gabriella had given me when I first asked.

"We do things like recovery of people and property, surveillance, and we even break into banks, sometimes." I got a grin from White with that one.

"That's not our complete resume, though," he added. "Sometimes we merely provide security for high profile people, such as yourselves."

"Break into banks?" Joel had the same reaction I did.

"Only to test the security," I answered much in the same way Gabriella had.

"So, do you all have military experience?" George asked.

"Most of our employees have a military background but not all of them."

"Special forces?" He pressed.

"Some, yes."

"You?"

"Navy SEAL."

"Can you tell us some stories?"

"Nope." White hiked his head to the side. "Shall we take a tour?" He asked me.

"I've already—"

The look on his face told me he was done talking to this crowd and so was I. He pointed to my champagne glass and Sydney brought one over for him and filled them both. He gave a little wave with his hand and she left the bottle next to the glasses. White handed me my glass, scooped up his own and the bottle, then led me away from all of the questions.

"I thought you didn't want them to know who we were," I said as we strolled across the deck.

"It couldn't be helped. Billy called you commander and they were all talking. I heard the plastic surgeon ask you what you commanded."

"She's quite—" I stopped and held out my glass for White to refill it. "Snobby."

"Where did you come up with that line back there?"

"What line?"

"The one about breaking into banks?"

"Oh." I laughed. "That's what Gabriella told me when I first applied for the job."

"Sounds like her." He nodded.

I found myself outside our room and started to feel a bit ill again.

"I thought you wanted a tour." I stated as he held the door open for me.

He shook his head. "Nah. We let them know that it's probably best to leave us be. And not showing our faces again tonight will add to the enigma."

I ducked under his arm and entered the room. My bag was just inside the door, so I went right to it for something other than my bikini. When I turned around I found White lounging on the bed in his wet swim trunks.

"I'm going to shower. Get off the bed and change your clothes. I don't want you getting the bed all wet. I have to sleep there, too."

"That's right." His devious grin returned.

The champagne and shot had made me tired and the hot shower did more to relax me. Actually, the alcohol had probably been a good idea because my mind performed gymnastics, thinking about White and sharing a bed with him. I reminded myself I'd slept next to White several times since we'd first met and we were on a job. Nothing would probably happen until after the job was finished, if at all.

When I stepped from the bathroom, White was still on the bed flipping through channels on the television. He'd changed from his swim trunks into a pair of flannel pajama pants.

"Your turn," I said and spread my swimsuit out to dry. "Dang it, I left my dress up on deck."

"Scott brought it down a little while ago." White pointed to the wardrobe where I found it hung nicely on a hanger next to White's shirt. They looked good together and I smiled.

I woke a few hours later and felt White in the bed next to me. I fought against a sharp intake of breath and stayed as still as I could. The room was dark and quiet, except for White's even breathing. I tried to go back to sleep but couldn't. After more than half an hour of being perfectly still I slowly slipped from the bed and left.

The gym felt like the safest place to be right now. If my thoughts were going to give my brain a workout I might as well give my body one, too. Why hadn't he tried anything? Maybe he wasn't going to. Maybe that was best. But, why hadn't he tried? Would I have given in? Yes, I would have. I jumped on one of the treadmills and started running.

"Early morning workout?" White's voice came up behind me. I almost fell off the treadmill before I could push the stop button.

"I couldn't sleep." I was breathless.

"You were sleeping just fine until about forty-five minutes ago." He closed in.

I looked at my bare feet and tried to get my breathing under control.

"Are you going to come back to the room or are you going to run all night?" He backed away slightly, allowing me room to walk past him.

I took the opportunity and led us back to the suite.

"You must be out of shape," he said as he shut the door.

"Why?"

"You're still panting from that short run." Again, he moved in close.

"It's not the run," I admitted quietly as I held my ground.

"Is that so?" He looked down and took my hands in his. Then he kissed the top of my head. I lifted my chin and looked him in the eyes. My heavy breathing had stopped and I held my breath.

White moved my hands to his waist and pulled me closer. He slowly traced a line along my jaw down to my neck. I took in a deep breath as he leaned down to kiss where his fingers had just been.

"Okay?" He asked quietly as his hands continued to roam.

I barely nodded before I felt his lips on mine. I was so caught up in him I didn't even realize we'd somehow made it to the bed until the cool pillow touched my head.

Chapter Three

I LAY ON MY SIDE STARING at the cabin's wall. A cool breezed drifted in through the open window causing goosebumps to rise up on my bare skin. White snuggled in closer, holding me tight. Even if it was incredibly relaxing and comforting to have White so close there was no way I would be able to sleep. More than an hour passed this way before White finally broke the silence.

"So." His voice was barely above a whisper. "What are you thinking about?"

I tensed. "I don't know. Us?" I couldn't tell him my real thoughts. I'd been analyzing every touch, every movement, over and over. Had I just made the worst mistake of my life? Had I just screwed up any future with White by my lack of experience? Just because I enjoyed myself doesn't mean he did. My stomach was in knots and I was fighting to keep my nervous shaking undetectable. How would I cope if he wanted nothing more to do with me? What if he never touched me again? What if he really was *mine* now? That was the scariest thought.

"Good." He held me a little tighter. "I'm actually thinking about that bikini. You look good in a wetsuit but that bikini—" He whistled.

"For a while I thought I might have to share the room with you and that bartender. What's her name?" The light tone put me more at ease.

"I don't remember. I think she's a client of Doctor Stoddard."

"I think so, too." I giggled. "And, so you don't forget again, her name is Sydney."

"I know," he admitted.

"Thought so." I nudged him with my elbow.

We lay still for several minutes more. The scent of White had always intoxicated me, and the feeling of his skin against me was almost paralyzing. It made me light headed and giddy. It pissed me off that I had no control when it came to White. Why did I let my libido make my choice? What the hell was I going to do now? Quit my job, get married and start having babies? No fricking way. I squirmed until he loosened his hold enough for me to roll to the edge of the bed. I leaned over the side to search for my clothes.

"Whoa." White pulled me back into his arms and I couldn't resist. Before I knew it, he mirrored my body with his own. His warmth seeped into me. "Where are you going?"

"I'm cold." My emotions were a tangled mess, and I didn't know which one was the right one. Exhilaration filled me, but so did shame, confusion and fear. I couldn't pick out which one was dominant.

"The morning-after weirdness."

"What?" I was waiting for his hold to loosen so I could squirm away and finish finding my clothes.

"That weird feeling when you wake up in the morning next to a new body," he explained.

"What do you mean?" I asked.

"You know. When it's hard to find something to talk about. You're wondering what the hell you just did and why. How are you going to get out of it?"

I remained silent. I didn't want to admit he was right, but I couldn't lie and deny it. What if I hurt him? Even if I wasn't ready to settle down, I didn't want White to give up.

"It's funny. You're the only woman I've not had that experience with. This feels normal and right." He moved his hand slightly down my leg. "But, I know you're feeling it because you're tense," he said.

"Fine," I said. "I'm feeling a little unsure."

"Why are you feeling unsure? If you have a good reason, get dressed and we'll pretend this never happened." He let go of me and put some distance between our bodies. I didn't dare move.

I knew why I was unsure, but I didn't know if it was a good reason. I couldn't give up what I had before we finalized the contract. Well, I *could* but I sure as hell didn't want to.

"I don't want anything to change." The heat on my back where White had been only moments before was fading, making me shiver.

"Me either." He replaced his arm around my waist and pulled me back into his body.

"I love my job," I said.

"I love *my* job," he repeated my words.

"I've wanted this for a long time." I pressed my head into his shoulder.

"How about we take it a day at a time?"

I nodded and sighed. "Sounds good."

"I suppose we should get dressed, anyway. We need to go over our plan. I just wanted to be sure this wasn't just a one time thing." White rolled away and started collecting his own clothes. I could hear the satisfaction in his voice. His admission that he worried I might not be in this for the duration gave me my own satisfaction. We dressed in record time and made our way to the small writing table against the wall.

White pulled out some paperwork from his pack and laid it out on the table.

"This photo isn't even a year old." He pulled a photo of Ruiz out of the pile. "The Admiral was more concerned with his current security detail, so we have to focus on them."

I nodded my understanding as White pulled out a satellite picture of the resort.

"I've asked the captain to anchor somewhere in this area." He circled a small area in the water. "We should have a great view, but still be far enough away from shore to avoid alerting anyone."

He pulled the paperwork back together. "If you want to go over anything else, you can find this in my pack." He held up the envelope before he put it away.

"That's it?"

"Yep. Short and sweet. This should be a simple operation. I'd like you to find out how many people Ruiz has in his party to make sure we get pictures of them all, but that should be simple and can be done when we get there."

"Oh, I already did that. He'll have six additional people staying at the resort with him."

"Good. Looks like we're all set." He glanced at the window. "The sun will be up soon. Were you going to go back to bed?"

"Actually," I looked at my watch. It read 4:39 AM. "I thought I'd go get some time in the gym before everyone gets up."

"Do you mind if I get a little sleep, then?"

"Of course not."

THE GYM WAS STILL UNOCCUPIED when I walked in. There weren't that many machines to choose from. A pair of treadmills faced the back wall that wasn't really a wall at all. It was a huge window that showed a great view of the ocean. I could still see the stars over the water even though the sky was starting to turn a light gray on the horizon. A pair of exercise bikes stood next to the treadmills and a monstrous multi-purpose machine sat in the center of the room.

The view made my decision on what equipment to use. The treadmill also had built in music system with ear buds. *Bonus,* I thought as I grabbed one of the sanitary wipes near the treadmill, wiped off the ear buds and put them in my ears. I ran to music, watching the sun light up the world and thought of nothing but White and what we'd done. Several times I wanted to get off the treadmill to go throw up but I ran through it and found myself grinning more than feeling sick to my stomach.

When my legs were about to burst into flames I slowed to a jog. My watch told me I'd been running flat out for more than forty minutes. I jogged until the searing sensation lessened to a warm burn then hopped off the treadmill. I'd forgotten the ear buds were attached to the treadmill and they were ripped from my ears. I felt foolish and spun around to make sure no one was watching.

Sam and Billy were at the multi-purpose machine. Sam let out a loud laugh and Billy wore a grin. I felt my face heat up. Thankfully, I'd not been singing out loud as I ran.

"Oh, shut up," I told them as I reached for a towel to wipe away my sweat. I dabbed at my face for a couple of seconds then started to wipe down the machine with the sanitary wipes, starting with the ear buds.

"The crew will take care of that after you leave." Sam grunted as he pushed up hard to lift the weights on the machine.

"If I do it, at least I know it's done," I answered and finished up the job. "What time do people start getting up?"

"You've got a couple hours yet. Why?" Sam stopped his exercises and walked toward me.

"I was thinking about a morning swim but I want the pool to myself, if possible."

"Use this one down here, then. Where's White?"

"I think he's still sleeping. At least he was when I came in here. Did you need him for something?"

"No, just wondering."

"You're sure? I'm going back to the room to change into my swimsuit. I could wake him."

"No. I'm sure he'll be up soon enough. I was asked to take him to the Captain later this morning, so it's not pressing."

"Okay, then. See you gentlemen later."

"Later," Sam said.

Billy had taken Sam's place on the machine and scrambled to stand at attention as I left.

WHITE WAS ASLEEP, SO I was as quiet as I could be while rummaging for my one-piece. I'd taken Gabriella's advice and brought three swimsuits as well as two wetsuits, the spring suit for warm water and a full body suit. As soon as I located the suit I turned to make sure White was still asleep. His features were softer than I'd ever seen them. He was so still I worried. I stared to make sure he was still breathing. He stirred a little. I didn't want to get caught gawking so I moved into the bathroom. At least I knew he was still among the living.

I pulled my hair into a braid as soon as I got out of the shower, and quickly put on my suit. I brought my damp towel out of the bathroom with me so I'd be sure to have one poolside.

White was sitting up on the bed when I exited.

"I'm sorry. Did I wake you?"

"No. It was just time to wake up." He smiled.

"Sam was looking for you."

"Already?"

"He said it wasn't pressing. Just that the Captain wants to see you later this morning."

"Waterstone must really want me up there with him. He asked me to come up yesterday and now he's got Sam searching me out, too. All he wants is help to plot his course. He doesn't really need me. I've already shown him where I want him to anchor for the week." He shook his head.

"Maybe he enjoys your company."

"He's an old friend of my dad's. They served together. He's a great guy, don't take me wrong. I'd just like to spend some time in the hot tub. Maybe do some fishing, or hang out in our room." He winked.

My heart skipped and my breath caught in my throat. I grinned in spite of my embarrassment. "I never thought of fishing." I tried to blow it off but White's smile became even broader.

"Going for a swim?" He still wore that satisfied grin.

"Yeah. I'm sick of that treadmill. Besides, Sam and Billy showed up and I didn't feel like working out with them in the room."

"I might see you in a little bit. I think swimming is probably the best exercise for me right now." He touched his scar gingerly.

Our exercise last night presented itself in a different light and I found myself sitting on the bed next to him, touching the scar. "Are you okay?"

"A little sore." His voice took on a slight whine and the sinful grin became tired, but his eyes twinkled. I'd fallen into his trap.

"You're just fine." I narrowed my eyes and resisted the urge to smack him. I started to stand but he grabbed my wrist and pulled me to him.

"It got you over here, though."

The roughness ended as soon as his lips met mine and he kissed me tenderly. "Good morning," he said as we parted.

I was too out of breath to reply and just smiled back at him. M hand found his and held on tightly before I gave him one more kiss.

"It's going to be hard not to touch you in public," he said as I stood up.

"You'll manage."

I DIPPED MY FOOT INTO the pool to make sure it was heated like the one on the deck above. I wasn't disappointed and dove in. I was in the middle of my seventeenth lap when I noticed I had company. Mr. Stoddard sat near the pool, watching me. It felt weird to think of him as *Mr.* Stoddard when he was so close to my age, but Scott hadn't told me his first name.

I didn't know how long he'd been there. I finished my lap before I stepped out of the pool, Scott's advice to steer clear of Stoddard upfront in my mind.

"Don't quit because of me," he said as I acknowledged him with a nod and a smile.

"No. I'm done."

"Most people swim an even number of laps," he said.

"I wasn't counting," I lied, but he'd obviously been there long enough to know how many laps I'd completed. My eyes found my towel near the chair he'd chosen to occupy. He immediately retrieved it and came toward me. His chest was puffed out and he obviously put some effort in how he walked. It was similar to my practiced walk I used when I wanted to make an impression and only slightly more masculine. I pictured him walking in slow motion and added a flip of his hair in my mind. I almost burst out laughing from the vision. He was laying it on thick.

"My name's Sean." He held out his empty hand. I let my attention wander from the towel to the offered hand long enough to give it a firm shake.

"Alex," I said as I reached for my towel with my other hand.

He pulled the towel just out of reach and kept a hold on my hand. "You really don't need to stop because of me." He looked me up and down suggestively. He was quite attractive and his attention might have been flattering had he been more refined *and* had I not known he was married.

Pig.

"On second thought, you can call me Ms. Grey." He let his grip loosen and his face took on an offended look. I, however, moved my grip from his hand to his wrist to give myself better leverage and make it easier to pull him in close. A smirk covered his face. It clearly told me he expected something other than what I had in mind. He placed my towel on my hip right along with his hand. Then he gave a slight tug, using my hip as a handle. He pushed himself harder against me. He was obviously trying to give me a taste of what I could expect after the clothes came off. It didn't evoke what I'm sure he hoped for. I shivered in disgust.

"You like to be in charge?" He breathed at me.

My nostrils flared, but I managed to keep my expression pleasant. I snatched the towel from his grasp. I wanted to throw him to the ground to show him how much I loathed being hit on by a married man, but instead, I pulled him closer and said into his ear "Thanks" in a sweet voice. Then,

I added, "You really should keep your hands and your wandering eyes to yourself. Consider this your only warning, *Mr. Stoddard* ."

I moved back a step and noticed his expression changed to anger almost instantly and his hand that had latched onto my hip dropped to his side. I didn't loosen my grip on his wrist and cocked my head to the side to challenge him.

"Stoddard isn't even my name. She made me take *her* name when we got married," he spat.

Any man who would become a trophy husband couldn't have much in the cojones department, but I'd hit a nerve. Even if his tone was whiny, his stance was that of someone ready to throw down.

"Your choice, your problem." I let go of him and stood my ground. The look on his face and his stance made me hesitate to turn my back on him.

After several long seconds of staring at me he finally backed down. "Sorry, Alex. I just thought we might have some fun."

"Ms. Grey."

"What?" he asked.

"You can call me Ms. Grey." I gave him a friendly smile. I was purposefully egging him on. I hadn't been in a fight for a long time and he'd pissed me off.

"Ms. Grey." He turned and walked away. Definitely lacking *cojones*.

I waited until he was a fair distance away and moved back toward my own room. Sam and Billy waited for me just outside the poolroom.

"Hi, guys," I said.

"I was hoping we'd have a fight to break up." Sam was disappointed.

"You saw that?" I pointed back to the pool.

"It's our job to police the ship, ma'am," Billy replied.

"Then why didn't you come help me?" I leveled at him. He shrunk a little at my question and looked at Sam. I turned my gaze to the superior officer.

"You can handle yourself, Commander." Sam stood at attention, looking straight ahead. "We would've been right there had he started to get the best of you."

"You think he might have gotten the best of me?" Now Sam was starting to piss me off.

"Not at all, ma'am. That's why we didn't interfere." His voice was calm and matter of fact.

"Oh." My anger was gone in an instant. "Okay, then." I lifted my chin and the men visibly relaxed.

"And I didn't have to grab your ass to get a good story to tell." Sam promptly returned to his relaxed demeanor.

"Keep it up and you might have two," I joked.

Chapter Four

WHITE WAS ALREADY GONE FROM from the room when I got back. Even so, I still did all of my preparation in the bathroom with the door locked because I knew he could come back at any moment. We'd spent an intimate night together, but I didn't want him to walk in on me.

Why?

If I planned to keep him, it wouldn't hurt to let him become very familiar with my natural state, but I just couldn't do it. I'd been guarding it for so long it was hard to give up.

When I was dressed for the day in my vacation attire, another cute and light dress with sandals, I pulled out White's packet on the target. I memorized all the info and replaced it. Then I rummaged through his equipment bag.

The most interesting piece was the digital camera and its several high-powered lenses. I was tempted to take it out of the room and act like a tourist. Instead, I put it away until I could ask White about it.

I wandered around the lower deck, looking for White. I was fairly certain he was up on the bridge with the captain but I checked everywhere below decks, just in case. Eventually, I made it up to the upper deck. The sun sparkled on the water and its warmth seeped into my shoulders.

I stood at the railing watching the water roll past. It was hypnotic and I drifted off into daydreams about White. We'd really been together. We'd sealed the deal. The anxiety of the past couple of months disappeared. I was content. Every second of last night, every touch, replayed in my mind. At that moment, I was ready to tell the world about us, and marry him if that's what he wanted. I don't know how long I spent in my trance before I noticed the noises behind me.

Sydney, the well-endowed bartender, prepared the bar for business. I must have missed breakfast. That thought made my stomach growl loudly.

The ache in my stomach threatened to expand, but I didn't see any way past that. I gave up my search for White and sought out the closest lounge chair to enjoy the warm sun. White would come find me when he had time.

"MS. GREY?" A SLIGHT TOUCH to my shoulder jerked me from sleep.

"Scott." Surprised and more abrupt than I wanted to be, I sat up straight and repeated his name with more control.

"I'm sorry, ma'am, but you might want to get in out of the sun. You've been napping on deck for a couple of hours now, and it's easy to get burned out here."

"Thanks, Scott." I sat up. "I hadn't intended to fall asleep out here." I looked around and realized the upper deck was bustling with activity.

Scott escorted me down the stairs with a light touch on my elbow.

"I feel foolish," I admitted.

"No need. Everyone naps on the upper deck and I have to regularly wake people to be sure no one gets sunburned. However, I'm afraid I got to you a bit late. You probably want to stay below decks for the rest of the day. More sun will just be harmful."

I hadn't noticed the tight feeling or heat until he said this. I glanced at my arms and was greeted with a pretty red color.

"Great." I sighed.

"Come with me. I'll get you some lotion."

"Thanks again, Scott," I said as I followed him below.

He unlocked the door to the cabin and I followed him inside. It wasn't as lavish as the room I shared with White and had a more lived in feel to it.

"Is this your cabin?" Surprise took hold and I hesitated just inside the door.

"Yes, ma'am. The sun cream is from my personal stores. I don't have to use it as much as I used to but I keep it stocked, just in case."

"Thanks for going out of your way for me." I accepted the bottle he handed to me.

"Absolutely, ma'am." He gave me a warm smile. "I don't mind going out of my way for you."

He followed me out of the cabin. "We missed you at breakfast. Lunch will be ready in fifteen minutes. Mr. White asked me to make sure you join him," he said.

"See you soon, then." I returned his smile.

My shoulders were stinging and my stomach was still protesting its hunger. When I entered my room I slathered on the lotion as quickly as I could and the cool feeling was a relief. Now it was time to do something about my stomach.

I was the first to enter the dining room and I watched Scott as he directed the crewmembers to their appointed tasks of readying the room for a meal. When I applied at White and Associates I had no idea what I was getting into and thought I might be applying for a similar job to what I was witnessing right now. At least I thought that until I started filling out all of the security related questionnaires. Not that this type of job would fill my need for adventure now that I'd had a taste of my current world, but this type of job had its perks.

"Is there anything I can do to help?" I asked as I watched them work.

I was met with confused looks and silence.

"Thank you, ma'am." Scott pulled out a chair for me. "The staff has it under control. If you'd like to take a seat I'd be happy to send out a plate." He disappeared into the kitchen.

"Shouldn't I wait for the rest of the passengers?" I asked under my breath as I reluctantly slid into the seat.

"No need," White's voice gave me a thrill. Goosebumps rose on my arms and a shiver accompanied them when his finger ran lightly across my shoulder. Even though this irritated my sunburn a bit, the feeling wasn't completely disagreeable. "Got a little sun, I see."

"Yeah. I fell asleep on deck."

He sat in the seat next to mine and said in a whisper, "Sorry to have kept you up so late."

I couldn't hold in the grin or fight the heat that rose to my face.

"The sunburn doesn't hide the blush as much as you might think." His seduction setting was set on maximum.

"Shut up, already," I said through my smile and clenched teeth. I took a deep breath and regained my composure just in time.

The staff delivered our lunch. I don't know what I expected but what I didn't expect was another four-course meal. We started with a chilled cucumber soup and they followed that up with a green salad. With the salad in front of me I asked White why we were still the only passengers in the dining room.

"I asked if we could eat earlier than everyone because I know you hadn't had breakfast and I might have said something about a private meeting."

"What are we meeting about, then?" I asked.

"I think Gary is going to keep me busy for the rest of the cruise to Jamaica and you're going to have to fend for yourself. I need you to remember that we are *employees* and we shouldn't instigate anything with the regular paying customers. Do you think you can avoid any more trouble?"

"*Instigate?* I did not *instigate* anything. All I did was let a pig know I wasn't interested in making his day. "

"Sam told me. I just can't have you fighting with the passengers. It was Sam's instinct to back you, but he really should have been concerned for the passenger. *That* is his job, to protect the passengers. But, now that Sam knows that, he won't be able to back you if something were to happen and I can't have you hurting Sam or Billy."

"The little pig is lucky he's still standing."

"Okay." He grinned. "I'm not faulting you for what happened, just asking you to try to avoid contact from now on."

"If the guy has any brains, he'll avoid me." I slid my plate away.

"Alex." He took my hand. "Don't be like this. I have to keep the peace. I understand where you're coming from but it's our job to protect the people on this boat, not injure them."

"I didn't touch him." I straightened my spine.

"Actually, you bruised his wrist." White's smirk quelled my temper some.

"So, the pansy bruises easily." I couldn't help but smile. "I'll avoid him as best as I can, but I won't lay down for him no matter how nice you ask me to."

"I'm definitely not asking *that* ." White's eyes narrowed. "I've already spoken to him. I know you won't have any more trouble from Stoddard, it's the other men on board I'm worried about."

"The other guys aren't married— Wait. You did what?" I pulled my hand from his. "Why did you do that? It just makes me look incompetent."

"No, it doesn't. I explained your position in the company and made sure Stoddard knows you are fully trained. He knows he was lucky to have walked away from that encounter with only a bruised wrist." He chuckled. "It was pretty funny, actually. He begged me to not tell his wife."

"He's sickening," I said and retrieved my salad just in time to have it removed for the next course.

We sat in silence through the main course but when our dessert came I broke the silence by making small talk about the camera. By the time we finished dessert we were past the tense moment caused by Sean Stoddard.

"I'm going back to the room," I said as the other passengers started to filter into the dining room. "I think it'd be best if I stayed out of the sun for the rest of the day."

"I probably won't see you again until dinner," he gave my hand a light squeeze before we left the table. My pulse quickened at his touch and my mouth went dry.

I smiled at him, pretending I'd already adjusted to our clandestine relationship. "See you later, then." I grinned all the way back to the room. White's semi-secret show of affection just made the flames grow higher.

I SPENT THE REMAINDER OF the day in the suite alternating between reading on my laptop and surfing the Internet.

As the sun set I decided to stretch my legs. I looked in the mirror and smoothed out my hair.

The doorknob wouldn't turn when I tried it. I let go to inspect it. Had someone locked me in my room?

I leaned down to check the knob the door opened in and hit me right on the forehead.

"Ow!" I stumbled back to the bed and sat down, rubbing my forehead while I kept my eyes squeezed shut.

"Alex! I'm so sorry." I heard White rush to my side. "Let me see. Are you bleeding?"

I took my hand away and inspected it. No blood.

I shook my head and took in a deep breath. I'd been holding it in and was getting light headed.

"You have a nice dent in your forehead." He tried to hide his amusement as he gently touched the spot. "What were you doing?"

"I was leaving to check on dinner and the knob wouldn't turn, so I was going to look at it."

He laughed. "At least you aren't bleeding."

I gave him an unappreciative look and he toned it down again. "I'm sorry. I had no idea. We just have good, or bad, timing."

"I guess." I rolled my eyes. "So, when is dinner?"

"I've asked that we be served in our room for the rest of the trip."

"Why?"

"Because, the less contact we have with the passengers, the better."

"I'm not going to cause any trouble." The pain in my forehead was getting worse and I was irritated.

"No. It's not you. We have some sensitive material to start going over, if we can. Plus," he hesitated a couple of seconds. "I'd rather spend time with you than Waterstone."

It had only been a day and I wasn't sure how to react to White's new display of affection. I looked at my hands and breathed in through my nose.

What do I do? Anxiety filled my stomach. I didn't know how to behave in a relationship. Should I just let the moment pass? Should I look up from my hands? The urge to give him a quick kiss and run away laughing was about to win until I pictured a couple of little kids doing that exact same thing on the playground. Instead, I took his hands in mine and leaned in and kissed him. He returned the kiss with more passion than I expected.

When we parted I asked, "So, what kind of material?"

"What?" He asked, the confusion thick on his face.

"You said we had some sensitive material to go over?" I reminded him.

"Oh, yeah." He took in a deep breath and let it out slowly. "I'll have to remember not to mention work to you when I'm hoping for something else. You have a one track mind at times."

"So do you," I answered.

"I can't help it. I'm a man."

"Whatever. That's the lamest excuse I've ever heard. You think I don't have desires?"

"I know you have desires. They're just more work related rather than entertainment related."

"You might be surprised," I said under my breath.

"Really?" He moved in closer and I studied our entwined hands. He touched my forehead lightly. "I think that might bruise." His kiss was gentle and light. He continued the kissing, making his way from my forehead down to my neck. I thought of protesting, citing work to be done, but I gave in and let the moment flood my senses.

A light tapping at the door shattered it all and White swore. I assumed it was dinner. I still hadn't caught my breath when White reached the door so I excused myself to the bathroom to calm down.

I leaned over the sink for several seconds. After taking some relaxing breaths I rearranged my clothing. A little less ruffled, I stepped from the bathroom to find our dinner waiting on a rolling tray near the table.

"Dinner, ma'am?" White pulled a chair out for me.

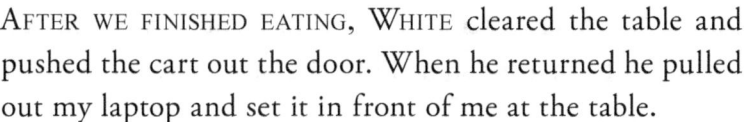

AFTER WE FINISHED EATING, WHITE cleared the table and pushed the cart out the door. When he returned he pulled out my laptop and set it in front of me at the table.

"I need you to do some research on Ruiz. I know I always say I don't care why the Admiral wants us to do things, but this time, I want to know. We'll be in position tomorrow and I want to be prepared."

"What exactly are you looking for?" I asked as I turned on the computer.

"The Admiral wants us to focus on the security detail, so I want to know who handles his security, if you can find that out."

"Okay." I started poking around, using my Penumbra access. White sat back on the bed and flipped on the television. One of the benefits of taking on the role of Penumbra, even in her off time, was the access I was granted to the government database. I think I had a higher clearance than even my father.

Mateo Ruiz's information was well documented and seemed current, except for his present security detail. According to the government database he'd dropped his long time security company about three months ago, but the company handling his security now wasn't on record.

I did find out Ruiz was suspected of having connections to the Medellin Cartel back in the day and the government also suspected him of trying to reestablish the organization.

"I can't find anything on his security. The government either hasn't updated who he's hired or doesn't know."

"I suspect they don't know and that's why we're on this mission," White replied.

"Did you know they think he had something to do with the Medellin Cartel and they also think he's trying to start it back up?"

"Yeah. I've known that for a long time." He came to the table and sat opposite me. "My dad was part of the intel team that tried to link him so we could extradite him. He never could find any real evidence." White took my pen and started writing on a piece of paper. "Let me help you."

When he finished he handed me the paper. "This is a list of possible security companies he might have contracted. Do you think you can get info about these companies with your laptop?"

"Probably. I don't know how long it'll take, though."

White moved his chair next to mine and I fought with myself to stay motivated to work. We spent the entire night going over the list but found nothing on record at any of the companies.

White yawned. "The sun's coming up."

"One of us should get some sleep," I said, stretching.

"We've slept in the same bed before."

"Yes, but things are different now and I'm afraid we won't get any rest. I'm going to go hang out with Sam for a few hours." I didn't hesitate getting a fresh change of clothes out of my bag.

"Fine. But, I did tell them that we had work to do, so it won't be strange if we don't show our faces again for several days."

I smiled. "You know that's not true."

"Okay." He gave in. "I only need a couple hours. Don't be gone too long. You need some sleep, too. We should reach our destination some time this afternoon."

IT DIDN'T TAKE ME LONG to find Sam and be granted permission to shadow him for the day. It was nice to visit with him and he kept his own distance from the passengers, so I was safe from making any more *mistakes*. White wasn't blaming me for Sean's behavior, even if it did feel like it. It just irritated me that I couldn't do anything I wanted because of Sean's stupid need to be unfaithful.

Several hours later I returned to the suite and quietly researched as White snoozed on the bed. According to the resorts records that I'd hacked into several times now, Ruiz had checked in around 11:00 AM the previous morning. I found the meal schedule and the man obviously liked to plan his days. All of his meals and that of his staff were already set up for his two-week stay. But, one interesting fact, Ruiz must have planned on a guest for lunch today because there were two special entrée's scheduled.

"Interesting," I whispered.

White's voice startled me. "What's that?"

"I'm sorry. I didn't mean to wake you."

"You didn't." White sat up.

"I thought I'd make sure our target and his security team would be at the resort when we show up in a couple hours. He checked in yesterday and even has all his meals scheduled."

"Sounds slightly interesting, I guess." White shrugged.

"The interesting part is that he has a guest for lunch today. Wonder who it is?"

"No idea. I'm sure this isn't purely a luxury trip for him. Ruiz rarely leaves Ecuador. Were you able to figure out where his security team is from?"

"Nope. I haven't been back to the room for very long."

"Okay. You should get some sleep. I'll wake you when we anchor."

"I'm not all that tired."

"We'll probably be doing some late night surveillance and I need you as alert as possible. Get some sleep. That's actually an order."

"An order?" I teased. I wouldn't jeopardize the mission in any way and I knew he was right, but I couldn't resist poking at him for his choice of words.

He took it seriously and said, "I'm not kidding, Alex. We can't afford to screw this one up."

"I *was* kidding." I climbed onto the bed and got comfortable as White walked out the door.

It seemed as if I had closed my eyes for only a few seconds when I heard the room door open again.

"We're anchored. This really is just a one man job, but you can come with me, if you'd like," White said as he readied his camera equipment.

"I'd like to. I still haven't gotten a chance to play with the camera."

"We won't be playing." He was all business now. "Get your wetsuit on. We're going out on the motor boat to look like snorkelers taking underwater photos."

"Sounds good." I pulled out my spring suit and changed in the bathroom and put my hair into a tight braid to keep it out of my way.

"Ready," I announced when I exited the bathroom.

White had on a similar suit to mine. He looked really good in it. It accented his muscular arms, legs and stomach. I smiled at him and raised my eyebrows suggestively.

He returned the look. "My thoughts, exactly."

I exhaled heavily as I walked past him and into the hallway.

"The Captain knows we're taking the boat. It's right back here," White moved toward the stern and down another set of stairs I hadn't had the chance to explore yet. It led us down to some more cabins. I assumed they were for the crew. Then, as we meandered down a little farther, Scott stepped from a doorway into the hall.

"This way, sir."

We followed him into the room, a nice sized bay with all kinds of watercraft. Billy was getting the boat out of the boat. This last thought made me giggle.

"What are you laughing about?" White asked.

"This is so cool."

White finally smiled. "Yes. It is."

The side of the yacht opened up and the motorboat slid out onto rails and was lowered into the water.

"So cool." I marveled.

Billy climbed down the ladder and into the boat and we followed. As soon as we were settled, he and White released the catches and Billy piloted us away from the yacht.

We took a few laps around the small bay and around the yacht to find the best location for our surveillance.

Eventually, Billy stopped the boat a good distance from the yacht and White readied the camera.

"Here," he handed it to me and dove off the boat. I watched as he surfaced and swam back toward us. He reached up for the camera. When he had it in hand he asked, "Are you going to join me?"

He didn't have to ask twice. I dove in over his head. The water was a beautiful blue and I could see the white sand through the water. I expected a little cold shock, but the temperature was perfect.

"Enjoying yourself?" White asked when I surfaced.

"Yep. You?" I wiped the water from my face.

"You have no idea." Again, he smiled at me. "I'll let you man the camera this time. Try to get good pictures of everyone. The Admiral likes front facing pictures as well as profile pictures."

I took the camera from him and zoomed in on the resort. I just hoped the water would remain calm so my pictures wouldn't be blurry. It didn't take long to locate the correct cabana. I scanned the entire area and located Ruiz and four of his security team immediately.

This is going to be easy.

Ruiz, another man and four of the six expected targets were all outside. The two men sipped drinks on the patio and four men stood guard in various places, surrounding the veranda. I snapped picture after picture and then moved my sites around the area again.

The two men I'd not accounted for yet soon relieved the men placed on either side of the door. One of them chewed on something. They probably eat in shifts. I snapped several pictures of them and told White, "I think I've got enough of all of them."

"All of them?"

"Yes, sir."

"Okay. Let's get back to the yacht so we can go through them and send them to the Admiral."

We swam the short distance back to Billy and the waiting motorboat. White climbed in first and offered me his hand as I climbed in behind him.

"Thanks." I plopped into my seat.

"If your pictures are good enough, maybe we can go inland tomorrow and do a little sight seeing," he suggested as he sat.

"Sounds great," I half shouted over the engine as Billy piloted back to the yacht.

I expected to go back to the side of the yacht where the boat had exited, but Billy moored us aft of the yacht.

"We aren't going to put it back?" I was disappointed. I wanted to watch them raise the boat back into place.

"No. I'm sure we'll use the boat tomorrow. Some of the passengers may even want to go out yet tonight." Billy answered.

"Come on, Grey," White's tone was impatient.

"Okay, okay." I followed him back to our room.

When we reached the suite, White opened the door for me. "You can relax while I download the photos onto the computer."

"But," I was going to argue that it was *my* laptop and I should do it, but his expression told me he was aching to see the results. I let it drop and went to my bag to get a clean change of clothes. I made my way to the bathroom to get out of my wetsuit and shower.

I'd just gotten my suit off when I heard White swearing and something crash into a wall. I grabbed my robe and held it up with one hand and threw open the bathroom door with the other. I expected to see White struggling with someone but he was madly pacing the floor alone.

"What's going on?"

He made two more laps around the room, then grabbed me by the arm and led me to the laptop. His grasp was firm but not painful. It was the yanking me along that made me almost drop my robe.

"These are the men you took pictures of today?" He stabbed his finger at the screen.

"Yes. What the hell?" I pulled my arm from his grasp. I watched the rage fade to embarrassment.

"I'm sorry, Alex." He sat down on the chair heavily.

"What the hell is wrong?" His gruff actions were forgiven and worry set in.

"I'm just—" he took a deep breath and seemed to regain his composure. He looked me directly in the eyes and said, "The Admiral should have told me that we might encounter these guys. They know who I am and it's possible we screwed up." His voice had a hard quality that I'd never heard before. He cleared his throat. "I didn't mean to grab you like that."

"I'm fine." I pulled the robe a little higher and wrapped it around my backside with my free arm.

"I'm still sorry," the remorse was thick. "You go finish your shower." He started flipping through the photos again.

I took the opportunity to slip into my robe.

"Who are these guys?" I wasn't fully convinced he'd be this upset just because they might have recognized us. "They weren't even paying attention to us." I said.

"I hope not." He shook his head.

I went back to the bathroom and just stood there for a few seconds, listening at the door. It remained quiet so

I turned on the shower and let the water run for another minute. When it still remained quiet I decided to shower for real.

After what was probably the quickest shower of my life, I dried off and got dressed.

When I stepped from the bathroom again, White was talking quietly on the phone. He'd taken the time to change out of his wetsuit. I got comfortable on the bed while straining to hear what he was saying. His voice was quiet and I wasn't going to be able to hear him so, I tried to position myself to watch his lips. He deliberately kept his back to me so I got up and moved to the table and sat opposite him.

"Now," was the only part of the conversation I got before he hung up. "Get packed. We're headed back to the mainland as soon as I can find Sam."

"I really don't think they even noticed us." I tried to reassure him.

"Probably not, but we absolutely can not be here any longer." He stood, walked over to me and kissed me on top of the head.

"I'm sorry we aren't going to be able to spend a little more time together. I had high hopes for this trip."

He didn't wait for my response and left me sitting at the table while he went in search of Sam.

LESS THAN AN HOUR LATER we set down in Miami and White was on the phone again. I said our good-byes to Sam and hurried after White.

I caught up to him just as he was hanging up his phone.

"Are you up for dinner at an airport restaurant? We've got some time to kill before Brown gets here." These were the first words he'd said, other than his most recent call, since we boarded the chopper back on *Carmen's Retreat* .

"Sure."

His demeanor still had me a little off guard and I wasn't ready to ask any more questions. It made me almost positive there was more reason for his attitude than a possibly botched op. But, I also understood White's strict position on *need to know,* and since he hadn't told me anything more, things were exactly as he had explained earlier or he thought I didn't need to know.

He chose the restaurant and picked a table with a full window view of the runways. White's outward mood had lightened, but there was a deep sadness in his eyes I'd never seen before.

Finally, I asked him, "What's really going on, Rick?"

He shook his head and sighed. "I might have really screwed up, Alex. The Admiral has been looking for one of those guys for years and if we were recognized—" He looked out the window.

I reached out and took his hand. His smile was gentle and full of gratitude. "Hopefully, our team will get there before the guy disappears again." He rubbed the back of my hand with his thumb.

"Dad should be happy to know you found this guy," I said.

"That's what surprises me. He's wanted this guy for years and if he had any idea that he'd be there, he should have told me. We could have sent in an extraction team instead of a surveillance team. He couldn't have had any idea." He was talking to himself now.

We sat only a few minutes more before White's phone rang.

"Yes. We're on our way."

Within fifteen minutes we were handing Black and Brown our luggage and gear to be loaded onto the plane.

"So? How did you like *Carmen's Retreat*?" Brown asked me as we all buckled in.

"It's gorgeous." That was the last of the conversation until I fell asleep in my seat.

I WOKE TO HUSHED VOICES coming from the cockpit.

"All I'm saying is that he's lucky it was her there with you," I heard Brown say.

"Our team should be there by now." Black's deep voice was unmistakable. "He can't hide any more."

The vehemence in his voice was something I'd never heard from Black. I *had* to figure out what was going on. When we got home I'd run the pictures through the government's facial recognition program and find out who the hell they were talking about.

"Hey, Alex!" Brown hollered a couple minutes later. "We're about to land. Wake up!"

"I'm awake!" I yelled back.

Chapter Five

THE FOUR OF US RODE the elevator down to my apartment. "I'll meet you two in the office in a couple minutes," White said as he stepped off with me on my floor.

He took my bags into my apartment for me and set them down just inside the door.

"I'm going to go meet with the Admiral right away. I don't know what he'll want to do, so I might be unreachable for a while."

"Okay," I expected this. I was aching to get onto my laptop to do my own research, but didn't want to hurry him off. Maybe there was a way I could help from behind the scenes.

He leaned down and kissed me. "Soon, though," he said and walked out the door.

My laptop was on my kitchen bar within seconds of White leaving but I couldn't find the pictures anywhere. I knew he'd put them on the computer, but he must have erased them. I searched in vain for almost an hour before I gave up.

I was okay with all of this when I thought I'd have somewhere to start my own research, but without those photos I didn't know what to do next. I began to pace.

After only three or four laps around my apartment I hopped back onto the bar stool and got into the governments facial composite program and started trying to piece together the men I'd seen. I did Ruiz first for practice because I remembered his face the best. It took me half an hour to get him put together and I transferred the composite over to the facial recognition program to see if it would pick the right guy.

While I waited on the results I started work on the rest of the men I'd seen. They were harder to piece together. If only I'd taken more time to study them, I kicked myself. Two hours later I finally finished one of the composites and transferred it to the recognition software. My piecing together of Ruiz had several hits. At least one of them was actually Ruiz.

I AWOKE TO A KNOCK at my door and realized I'd fallen asleep at my kitchen bar. How I'd stayed in the chair was a mystery. The knock came again, so I closed my laptop and went to the door.

"Everything okay?" Black asked as he stepped past me into my apartment.

"Yeah, why?" I rubbed some sleep from my eyes.

"You're still wearing the same clothes from last night." He was looking around my apartment with a suspicious look.

"I fell asleep at my computer." I yawned. "What time is it?"

"Five-thirty. Thought you might like to join me at the gym." His roving eye seemed satisfied and he addressed me directly.

"Yeah. I could do that. Can you give me a minute to get changed?"

"Sure," He went to my kitchen bar and sat.

I picked up my laptop from in front of him and went to my bedroom to change. I tossed it on the bed. It did a couple of little bounces, making me worry that it might not have been a good idea to toss it. When it didn't hit the floor I hurriedly dressed. Then, I took a brief look at where I'd left off last night. I fought the urge to swear. I had almost one thousand possible candidates to weed through for one of the composites and I still hadn't even finished all of them. I'd have to deal with that when I got back.

HELIX'S GRUFF AND DIRECT SPEECH made me as uncomfortable as always.

"You got some sun, girl." He wagged his eyebrows. "Is it an all over tan?"

"No." I wanted to scream at myself for actually answering that question. Now he had facts to back up his imagination.

"I prefer tan lines. There are some places that the sun shouldn't kiss. That's better left up to a good man."

I felt my face heat up and let my eyes wander around the gym instead of looking at Helix or Black.

"I love how innocent you are." His laugh boomed across the gym.

"Maybe it's not innocence, but being a lady."

Black always came to my defense when it came to Helix. Maybe that was why I allowed Helix more room, I always had a champion in my corner to protect me. Plus, I thought most of what Helix said to me was somehow directed at Black.

"Ahh." His grin lost most of the wolfishness. "I suspect we might both be right," he told Black as the two of us walked away.

"Why do you let him get away with that?" Black asked as we sparred.

"I really don't know," I answered as I dodged his huge fist he thrust at my middle.

If Brown had said anything like that to me, he would have gotten an earful. I didn't know why I couldn't stand up to Helix. Maybe it was because he was a friend of Black's and I was afraid of offending Black by offending Helix.

We didn't speak again until we were heading back home in Black's SUV.

"So, White said he knew the men I took pictures of. Who were they?"

"Some guys that used to work for another PMC based out of the city," he answered.

I might not have to spend days building composites and weeding through pictures.

"What PMC do they work for?"

"They don't. Not any more."

"Is there anything I can do?"

"No. This is the Admiral's problem. White turned it all over to him last night."

"But—"

"No buts, Grey. This is one you don't want to mess with." His jaw clenched shut and I knew I'd gotten all I could get from him. The use of Grey instead of Alex wasn't lost on me either. He rarely called me Grey anymore, unless we were involved in something for work.

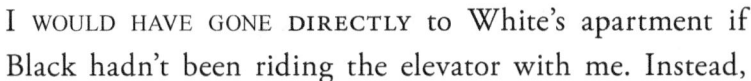

I WOULD HAVE GONE DIRECTLY to White's apartment if Black hadn't been riding the elevator with me. Instead,

I went back to my own apartment and showered before I rode the elevator back down to White's floor.

He didn't answer his door, so I rode down one more floor to the office.

Gabriella wasn't at her desk yet, but White was at his. He looked like he hadn't slept.

"Have you been up all night?" I asked.

"Yeah. I've been making sure we didn't have to do any damage control. There's no indication we were spotted."

"Are we going back for an extraction?"

"No. Your dad was grateful for the tip, but assured me he'd take it from here." I wanted to ask him why he erased the surveillance pictures from my laptop but he sounded exhausted.

"You should go get some rest." I said instead.

"I was about to." He stood.

When we stepped into the elevator I asked, "So, what's next?"

"With the job?" He took my hand.

"Everything."

The elevator door opened up to his floor.

"Let's talk in my apartment." He gave a slight nod to the elevator camera.

HE LET ME IN FIRST but as soon as he had the door shut he took me into his arms and held me close for a few long seconds.

"I'll try to find some time for us to be alone, soon. I promise."

"It's not going to be easy."

"No. It's not."

"Do you have any jobs lined up?" I moved the conversation forward.

"Nope. Well, nothing for you at the moment."

I couldn't stand it any longer. "Why did you take the pictures off my laptop?"

He raised his eyebrows at me. "I figured you'd check things out. That's why."

"If I'm not supposed to know, why did you even let me go on the op?"

"Because, I had absolutely no idea we'd find what we did. Your dad wasn't pleased when he found out you and I did the surveillance."

"Aren't I a part of this company? This need to know bullshit has gone far enough. Do you really think you can't trust me?"

I was not looking forward to building more composites and sifting through thousands of potential suspects. I was looking at, possibly, hundreds of hours of research.

"Alex. It's not like that."

"Really? What's it like, then?"

"It's a military matter." I grew up knowing that statement and anything like it meant there was no way I was going to get any more info unless I went back in time and was part of the mission it pertained to. Even though I respected *need-to-know* had a legitimate purpose I couldn't help being irritated that I wasn't in on the secret.

When I didn't continue to argue, White asked, "Promise you'll leave this one alone?"

I pinched my lips together and shook my head. "I can't *promise* ."

He stared at me.

"I'm sorry. I can't. I'd love to, but I really want to know and I can't promise. I don't want to break any promises I'd make to you."

"Alex—"

"Fine. What if I promise to *try* to leave it alone."

My shoulders slumped after I said this. This was almost as good as promising to never think of it again. The urge to run back to my apartment and continue researching was stronger than ever.

"You better keep me busy until this urge passes." I scowled at him.

"I'll find something to keep you occupied." His evil grin found its way past the drawn, exhausted look.

"After you get some rest." I smiled. "I'm going back to my place for a while. I haven't had much sleep these past few days, either."

I turned to leave and he grabbed my hand. He turned me around and pulled me in closer. His kiss was strong but didn't carry the hunger our previous kisses had. Instead, it conveyed a deep feeling of contentment and security and was, in a way, the most perfect kiss we'd shared.

Back in my apartment I stood in the door of my bedroom, staring at my laptop on the bed. I should delete everything pertaining to the op from the laptop. The photos that had popped up from my search started filling my mind and I tried to pick the right one from memory.

"Stop it," I said aloud and walked away from the bedroom. Instead of the bed, I napped on the couch.

When I woke I shuffled around my apartment for about an hour. I loaded the dishwasher and gave my bedroom a glance. Then I swept the linoleum in the kitchen and caught myself looking at my bedroom again. I did several other small chores for about an hour before the call of the laptop became too much.

Again, I stood in my bedroom doorway and stared at it. The damn thing was still where I'd left it. I gave in and went to the bed and picked it up. When I opened it, the pictures flooded the screen.

I closed them all out and put all the info into its own folder. Pressing the shut down command wasn't as hard as I anticipated. Then I took the machine and shoved it deep into my closet and dropped some clothes on top of it in a heap. If I couldn't bear to part with the photos then I'd have to part with the laptop until I could delete the info. My last step to beat the temptation was to ride the elevator down to the office.

Gabriella was at her desk and White's office door was shut.

"Hey, Hon!" She stretched her arm out to indicate my seat in front of her desk. I'd spent so much time in that chair the past month or so I swear it had my butt print permanently embedded.

"So? You're nice and tan." Her grin was broad.

"What did you do while we were gone?" I skirted her unanswered question.

"Nope. You first."

"Tell me what you did, first. I'll get us coffee." I got up, grabbed her cup and was pouring within seconds.

"Just came to work, went to dinner with Martin and spent the rest of the time cuddling with him on the couch. Now, spill."

She didn't mean the coffee I was bringing back to her desk.

"Is he in?" I asked with a hike of my head toward White's closed office door.

"Yep. In a meeting."

She held up one finger and wagged it at me. "Now. Back to it, girl. Did you have fun?"

"It was—nice."

She squealed. "Wait." Her eyes narrowed and she cocked her head to the side. "What does *nice* mean? Did you or didn't you?"

I hated her directness at times. I wanted to tell her, but White and I had agreed to keep it to ourselves, for now.

I spent the next half an hour chatting about everything else about my trip. I told her about Sean Stoddard's advances, the beauty of *Carmen's Retreat* and described the little bit of Jamaican scenery I'd seen in great detail.

"I wish I could have gone." She sighed. "But, you still haven't cleared up anything for me."

Just then, White's office door opened and my father and Master Chief Slade stepped out. They both looked as haggard and tired as White had earlier that morning.

"Dad?" I stood, a little shocked to see him in this state. "Master Chief."

"Hi, darling."

"Ms. Grey," Slade said and swiped his hand across his eyes as if to wipe away the fatigue.

"Been keeping busy?" Dad's shoulders still slumped, but he'd straightened them some for my benefit.

"Yes, sir."

This was not the place to start asking questions. Plus, I'd promised White. Chances are, the Admiral wouldn't be as gentle or understanding on this subject as White had been.

"I'll walk you out," I said and opened the office door for the men. I knew there would be no more conversation but I took this as an opportunity to walk away from Gabriella and her pressing questions. I rode down to the lobby with them in silence. It was uncomfortable, but not as uncomfortable as dodging Gabriella would have been.

Chapter Six

THE NEXT THREE DAYS WERE almost unbearable. I didn't sleep well with the laptop in my closet. Every morning I dragged myself out of bed barely in time to get ready to go to the gym with Black.

Through my tired haze I noticed Helix was more subdued and polite. I wondered what had changed.

Every morning after my workout, I'd go sit across from Gabriella and watch my partners come and go from White's office. White didn't call for me to be part of any of these meetings. That didn't stop me from showing up, hoping I'd get into one of the meetings. Gabriella had taken the hint and quit pressing me so hard for details about my Jamaica trip. On the fourth morning the traffic in and out of White's office stopped and I was sulking in my chair until she asked, "He hasn't called?"

I pried my eyes from his closed office door and shook my head.

"Ms. Grey's here to see you." She said into the intercom before I could stop her.

"Send her right in." I'd missed his voice.

I gave Gabriella an unappreciative look and said, "Why did you do that? Now what do I do?"

"I'm *not* going to stand for him pulling a hit and run," she snapped. "Ask him if that's what it was, that's what you're going to do."

I knew in my heart that this was not what was going on, but I couldn't help but worry about it anyway. The past three days had been torture, not hearing anything from White.

"He's just been busy." I told her. "Besides, we never—" I stopped myself before I completed the lie.

"Don't make excuses for him. And don't feed me a line of bull. *And* , don't let him feed *you* any shit."

I took a deep breath and stepped into his office.

I still didn't know what my excuse was going to be when he looked up and asked, "What's up?"

"Nothing. You promised to keep me busy." It was lame, but all I had.

"I know. Working on it. Actually, I'm glad you came down today. I was wondering—. I was wondering if I could talk you into going out on a date."

My stomach flipped, my face flushed and I felt ill. "Uhh," I stammered. *Just say yes!* I screamed at myself. Did this mean he wanted to make our relationship public? I wasn't sure how I felt about that.

"I mean, it's a favor to me and not a paying job but you'll get a good meal out of it." White quickly put in.

"A job?" I was visibly taken aback and tried to compose myself.

"Yeah. The client," he paused again. "He's not really a client. He's actually an informant or could even be called an operative. Anyway, he specifically asked for a date with you as payment for some recent information he delivered. He likes to be treated to a good meal from time to time and I guess this is one of those times."

"Who?" I was beginning to resemble Black with my one and two word responses.

"All you need to know is that you are to meet a Mr. Johnson for dinner. Have a good time and then come home."

"Who is *Mr. Johnson* ?" I had apparently crashed back to earth because my brain kicked into work mode. If I were going to do a job I should know as much about it as possible. This Mr. Johnson must know me to specifically ask for me. I wanted to know who he was too.

"I'll expect you back down here at six-thirty tonight. Your reservations are for 7 o'clock." He skirted the question and was already shuffling papers on his desk. I was a little dumbstruck so didn't react immediately. When he didn't acknowledge me again, I left his office.

"What did he say?" Gabriella waited until I shut the door.

"I have a date tonight," I said stiffly.

"Why is that not a good thing?" She narrowed her eyes.

"It's not with White."

"What? That makes no sense."

"It's a job."

"I told you not to let him get away with this. Did you ask him about the two of you?"

"No. He didn't give me the chance." I was getting angrier as the conversation progressed. "I'm going home for a bit." The compulsion to storm out of the office was strong but I resisted.

Back in my apartment a tear roll down my cheek as I looked at the closed door.

How could he do this to me?

I resisted the urge to run to my bed, throw myself down and bawl like a baby. I wiped the tears away and paced instead. This development only made me want to break my promise on purpose.

I'd go on his little date with the unknown Mr. Johnson because it was my job. I couldn't let my hurt feelings interfere with my work. White losing all respect for me had been one of my concerns about starting up an intimate relationship with White. Now I was right in the middle of one of my fears.

I PULLED OUT THE LAPTOP and spent the rest of the morning compiling composites of the men I'd seen.

Best to get it down before I forget the details.

Guilt ate at me with every bit of progress I made on the composites. I reasoned this wasn't really cheating. He didn't know how far I'd gotten and there was no harm in getting the computer-generated sketches on the laptop. I just wouldn't input them into the database. I only had a couple left to do, anyway. When I was done I replaced the laptop with a sick feeling. I'd broken my promise, but I felt a need to get even. But, I only did some sketches and not found out any real information, I didn't really do anything wrong. My excuses didn't make me feel any better about what I'd done.

I had to get out of my apartment and away from that laptop. I went grocery shopping. I had plenty of room in my refrigerator and cupboards. It didn't take as long as I'd hoped so when I got home I took my time putting the groceries away.

Still I had lots of time to kill before my *date*. I decided to catch up with phone calls. Mom was first on my list of two people. It didn't take long to get each other up to speed since we both were guarded with what we told each other. Not that we didn't have a good relationship, just that we both knew there were things in our lives that couldn't be discussed. At least in my life. As far as I knew, my mom had *retired* from her cloak-and-dagger way of life. The *need to know* even filtered into my relationship with my mother and I wondered why I wasn't used to it yet. I'd had plenty of practice being on the doesn't need to know list.

I refilled my cup with fresh coffee and went back to the phone to call Colin. He'd become more and more reserved in our conversations since he'd been promoted. I tried to figure out the source of his restraint but couldn't put my finger on it. Since he'd become more involved in my life, by being groomed to take my father's place with White and Associates, he seemed to want less to do with my social side than my occupational side. Needless to say, I wasn't really looking forward to trying to talk with him at this point, but I needed the distraction.

I took a deep breath and reached for the phone. After a short wait on hold, Colin answered my call.

"Alex? Is everything okay?"

"Yes. I just thought I'd call to catch up."

"I don't really have time right now. Can I call you tonight?"

"No. I have a date tonight."

"A date? With *whom*?"

"I don't know. It's a blind date and actually, it's really a job disguised as a date."

"Sounds like fun. Anything else?"

"Anything else? Are you really that anxious to get off the phone with me? We haven't talked forever and every time I call you don't even care what I'm calling for, unless it's work related." My self-pity made me lash out at Colin. Though, it was something I needed to say.

"Come on, Alex." He was angry now too. "You know I'm busy. This job of your dad's is not easy!" He sighed when I didn't reply.

Colin hardly ever raised his voice to me. White's inattention so soon after we'd sealed the deal had me in knots and Colin was the one who was always supposed to be there for me. I didn't trust my voice to remain even, so I didn't respond. I hated it when I cried, but I really hated it when I cried and other people knew about it.

"I'm sorry, Alex. I'm really stressed. I'm still learning how to balance it all."

"That's okay. I just miss you." I succeeded in keeping most of the sorrow from my voice.

There was a long pause then Colin said, "I miss you too. You don't know how much. I'll set aside some time for us real soon. I promise. I'd come by tonight, but you have a date."

"No, that's all right. I know you're busy and so am I. I'm just feeling sorry for myself right now. I'm really sorry I called you to yell at you."

I never stayed mad at Colin long and he was very forgiving of me too. We had the perfect friendship, most of the time. We could ignore each other for months and then pick up right where we'd left off. When we were kids, I assumed I'd marry Colin. He was all I knew, but as we grew older we agreed to keep our relationship platonic. Being friends was the most important part of our lives.

"I know I don't seem to give much consideration to your situation. You've got a more stressful job than I do. Do you have any new jobs lined up?" I knew he was referring to Penumbra. Colin was one of the few who knew. He'd never been told straight out but he'd been involved in some of the contracts and it was impossible to hide the facts from him. If he hadn't been a friend, he wouldn't have known I was out of town every time Penumbra was on a job, but I completely trusted him with the information, even if I would never physically say the words "I am Penumbra," to him. And, he would never ask, either.

"No. I think that's part of my problem. I'm going a little stir crazy."

"I can't even begin to fathom what you've been going through lately. And, frankly, I don't want to. I worry about you, out there. Working with White and his bunch is bad enough, but…" he left it hang. Then he put his hand over the receiver. I heard him tell someone, rather gruffly, "Not now."

"Sorry." He came back on the line. "I don't get any time for anything anymore."

"Thank you for being my friend, Colin. I should have realized you've been under a lot of pressure too. I suppose I better let you get back to work—"

"No, Alex. You are right. We should talk more. I've already told them I'm not to be bothered for a while, so let's talk. I know you can't tell me much of what you've been doing, and I can't really either. But, we had things to talk about before we got our new jobs. Maybe that's what we both need."

Colin had always been easy-going and somewhat immature, but this new job had turned him into a responsible man, almost instantly. He was still the guy who'd taught me sign language and how to read lips and who I'd spent countless hours with, eaves-dropping on people from a distance and partying with in the bars, but he didn't have the time for that anymore.

The long awaited conversation started out with small talk and I seriously debated about telling him about White. I really wanted to talk to him about it. I'd almost come right out and told Gabriella, why couldn't I tell Colin? As friends went, he was my first and best friend and I should tell him. The agreement to keep it secret for now was something I wanted to honor, but I really needed to talk to someone.

"So, what's got you so upset?" He finally asked.

"I've started dating a guy and he's not called me for four days." I pouted. Maybe I could talk to him about this and not mention names.

"Really? You haven't had a boyfriend since Anthony. Who is it?"

"No one you know." I hated to lie.

"If he hasn't called, move on," he advised.

"But, I really like this guy and he does have a good excuse for being absent. I'm just feeling left out of his life at the moment."

"You must really like this guy," he said.

"I do."

He sighed loudly. "I really don't know what to say to you. I've only been in love with someone once in my life and I will always be in love with her. If you're truly in love with the guy, I imagine it'll be the same for you, even if you don't get to be with him." His voice was halting and troubled.

"I'm sorry I dumped on you."

"No. Don't be sorry. It's about time you talked to me about something with actual meaning. It's been a long time coming."

I was feeling foolish for acting like such a girl until he said this. Maybe he was right. Maybe it was time to strengthen our bonds by confiding more in each other. I told him this and thanked him for listening.

"I'm sorry I can't give you advice on this. Actually, I could, but I won't. You already know my thoughts on you and White in a relationship."

"I didn't say it was White," I tried to sound offended.

"Who then? He's the only one you've been spending all your time with. When did you find time to fall in love with anyone else?"

"It's *not* White." I lied again and this time I tried to believe my own words.

"Well, who ever this guy is, he's lucky. Just remember, you come first and if he can't make time for you, he doesn't deserve you."

"Which one did *you* actually fall in love with?" I remembered all of Colin's girlfriends and wanted to know

.C. PHELPS

which one had stolen his heart. "Was it the hair-dresser? You know, the one who didn't know how to cut hair? Remember? Her hair was like five inches longer on one side than the other side."

"That was the style. Still is."

"What *was* her name?"

"I can't remember. That was right after high school."

"How about that other one? The one who snorted when she laughed. And she laughed at *everything* ."

Now I was giggling. Picking on Colin about his choice of women had always been one of our favorite past times. He pretended he didn't like it, but I never picked on a girlfriend, much, until after they had split. I'd had to deal with many a comment about Anthony and knew that would be the route the conversation would take next.

"At least this new guy is going to give me some new material. Anthony has become boring. But, remember when you tried to tell me how good he was at darts? I cleaned his clock and I'm not a very good player."

"Yeah, Anthony's an embarrassment."

It continued like this for a few more minutes until we were both satisfied the other was sufficiently cheered up. Then we said our good-byes with promises to get together soon. Before he hung up the phone I quickly called his name.

"Colin?"

"Yes?"

"Thank you."

"Any time." With that we both said goodbye one more time and I hung up my phone. Then, I realized he'd never answered my question.

I'D MANAGED TO KILL SOME time and I certainly felt better about my current circumstances. Colin, as always, had reminded me of who I was and I mattered to someone.

Gabriella had told me before, 'Sometimes there's nothing better than a good cry with a good friend.' She usually said this after a little spat she'd had with Martin and cried to me. The first time this happened I didn't know what to do and felt terribly uncomfortable. But now, after *a good cry* with Colin I better understood where she was coming from. I just hoped he didn't think of me as a big baby now.

Maybe I should forget White and go find a nice, calm man. The problem with that was I didn't want a nice, calm anything. That was most of White's appeal. He was anything *but* tame. He was confident, experienced, dangerous and unpredictable. It was the unpredictability that worried me the most. He could change his mind about me at any second. Who knows, he could already be over me.

Something Gabriella had tried to drill into my head was to get over my romantic notions that sex was anything more than sex. Yes, it was the bringing together of two bodies, but that didn't mean I had to release my heart and soul to the man, or men, I decided to play around with. That thought literally made me sick to my stomach. Maybe I wasn't ready for that yet, but that didn't mean I shouldn't be confident enough to sleep with any man that I felt like sleeping with, even if it was just a one-night stand. Again, a shiver of nausea radiated through me. Yeah, too soon to start thinking about sleeping with the whole city. I wasn't ready to replace White in my daydreams. There was no way I was ready to replace him in my bed.

Why am I thinking like White was just a one-night-stand? He'd never given me any indication of that. It's only been four days, I reminded myself. I was competent and suspected that was part of what White found attractive about me. I could handle myself. So, why did I even need to worry about a man? Hell, I was probably *the* most dangerous woman on the face of the planet, besides my mother. If it turned out White didn't want to continue our relationship, then so be it. It was his loss and possibly my gain.

I concluded it was best to just remember who I was and leave it at that. *I could kill you... just like that. And I'd get away with it too!* I openly laughed at myself.

I wouldn't let this fake date bring me down.

Chapter Seven

THE REMAINDER OF THE DAY was easier to pass and I started getting ready a little early. I pulled an emerald green, full-length gown from my closet and stepped into it. I'd bought it specifically to wear in front of White, hoping it would tempt him into a marriage proposal or something. Now he'd get to see me out on a date with another man in the dress I'd bought specifically for him.

I inspected myself in the full-length mirror, practicing those precise movements that allowed the long slits down the sides to reveal the lace on the top of my stockings for a seemingly accidental glimpse. It had been a while but the movements came back to me easily. I'd perfected them shortly after buying the dress. I could control every aspect of the gown to show what I wanted, when I wanted to.

Getting dressed was the easy part of the ritual of primping. My hair was a different story. I usually wore it in a ponytail or a braid to keep it out of the way but a date required a more provocative style. Even though this wasn't a true date I needed to be convincing. I stood in front of the bathroom mirror for thirty minutes trying to manipulate my hair into the perfect do. Finally I decided on a messy bun at the nape of my neck and curled the loose hair to give it more class.

Now for the shoes, I sighed loudly. To me, the shoes are the most important part of an outfit. I knew which pair I would wear before I put on the dress, but I had to fight myself to actually put them on.

I love high heels. They make me feel sophisticated and sexy, but I was ill at ease when wearing them. Shoes had to be functional in my line of work, but for a date it was more important that they match my ensemble. I buckled them loosely in case I had to remove them quickly. I hoped nothing would come up, but it wouldn't be the first time I had to go barefooted so I could actually move.

Going back to the full-length mirror I double-checked my special moves with my heels on. For some reason it was easier to achieve the right effect with the shoes. I admired myself in the mirror until I was satisfied. I made sure the choker I'd worn to a previous job was positioned correctly over my throat while I walked toward the elevator. It contained a microphone and GPS tracking device so my partners could hear what was going on and, if need be, find me. I hadn't been told to wear it, but it went well with the outfit and I had learned from previous experiences it wasn't always a bad idea to make sure I could be located. The only other item *Ms. Grey* had that had the GPS device was the company issued watch that would look extremely out of place with my current threads.

If I were doing this job as Penumbra I might use some sort of GPS but nothing the partners would be able to track. The need to know phrase jumped back into my head at the thought of Penumbra. Penumbra knew everything and Ms. Grey followed orders. Thoughts of what had been going on these past few days filtered back into my brain and I decided to ask White to be put on a job, any kind of job. I'd rather do a Penumbra job to feel more in control, but anything to get me out of here for a while was probably exactly what I needed.

THE ELEVATOR DOORS OPENED TO reveal an anxious White waiting to get on. His expression was one of irritation until the doors were fully open. Then he softened for a full second as he hesitated to get aboard. I'd become adept at judging his mood. Any show of emotions from White, other than anger or irritation, were minute and generally lost to all but the most observant.

"Well?" I cocked my head to the side, indicating the elevator.

His attitude changed back to one of annoyance.

"At least your tardiness has a reason." I caught the flare of his nostrils and a fleeting smirk of praise before he stepped in and faced the doors.

I fought myself to keep the smile of satisfaction from my face.

I love this dress.

"Are you driving me?"

"Yep." He didn't elaborate.

"Where are we going?" The pleasure from White's reaction to my dress was wearing thin and I was beginning to get irritated.

"You are going to Donatello's."

Finally, I was getting some answers.

"And?"

"As per your previous instructions, you'll ask to be directed to your reserved table," he paused and looked at me. "Table for two, under Johnson."

A couple of seconds passed as I waited for him to continue and when he didn't I let out an exaggerated sigh. "Do I have to drag it out of you or are you going to brief me?"

"You have been briefed."

The elevator doors opened up to the lobby. White put one hand on them and waited for me to step out before he followed closely behind.

"Ms. Grey?" Phil, the head of security for the building, was at the lobby desk. His voice was filled with doubt.

"Yes?"

"You look very nice." A flush crept into his face. He must not have recognized me in my date costume. It was painfully obvious I didn't dress up enough anymore.

Mr. Black had cautioned me against flaunting my womanhood in a company full of men but I still needed to remind them once in a while I was different than them and White needed to be reminded most of all. Being a woman, I should be a mysterious creature to them. Not just their partner and another one of the guys.

When I joined the company, all I wanted was to be one of the guys but now I wanted more recognition for being a woman as well as one of them. No one seemed to notice my femininity and I vowed to take more interest in my appearance from now on.

"Thank you," I told Phil as we exited the building into the parking garage.

White led me to his Mustang and opened the passenger door for me. For a fleeting second I thought maybe he was actually going to take me out on a secret date.

"Who is Mr. Johnson?" I pushed the subject.

"You'll see." I thought I sensed a hint of glee in his tone.

"Why are you driving me? I could have taken a cab." The hope that he had this planned for us was still there.

"I wanted to make sure you'd get there on time. Besides, it's the least I could do since I set you up on this date."

"So, who is this Mr. Johnson again?" I tried to trick him into telling me.

"You'll find out."

"Well, since I'm going to find out, why not tell me now?"

"I'm sorry, Alex, but it's better if we keep it simple."

"Keep it simple?" I let out an unattractive grunt. "This seems to be very complicated for keeping it simple."

White sighed. "Okay, you're right. Johnson specifically asked for you and you're doing me a favor by going on this date with him. It was really hard to turn him down now that we've started our own secret relationship. I wanted to turn him down without even talking to you but, I didn't want anyone to get suspicious. I couldn't give him a good reason why I wouldn't even bring it up to you. You accepted, so you're going."

"I'm going to regret this, aren't I?"

"No, it's me that will probably regret it."

Again, I thought I sensed amusement in his voice.

I HALF EXPECTED WHITE TO open my door after we pulled up to the restaurant so I hesitated for a second or two before I stepped out.

"I'll be back to pick you up later," he said before I shut the door.

Inside the building I did my routine scan of the people, exits and possible weapons lying about. I made sure I was satisfied before I asked about a table for two under Johnson.

The man leading me to my table couldn't have given any thought to my high heels as he swiftly maneuvered through the restaurant with me in tow. He led me to a quiet corner table and left me to wait alone. The third time I caught myself looking at my bracelet to check the time I smacked my wrist, as if it was the bracelets fault it couldn't tell me how long I'd been waiting. It was strange, when I was on a sniping mission, waiting was almost all I did, but somehow I didn't even notice. However, put me in a situation like this, and five minutes felt like five days. Eventually, my companion arrived.

When he walked in the door I knew why White had been so evasive. Helix was led to my table just as deftly as I had been.

I stood to greet him and was pulled into an unwanted embrace. He held on tightly as he breathed into my hair. "Mmmm, I knew you was fine, girl, but I didn't know you was *this* fine."

I liked Helix but he was much too forward for me to be comfortable. His hot breath made me cringe but the thought dominating my brain was the suit he wore. Helix was a huge man and I had no idea he could even fit into a suit. Had I ever taken the time to picture him dressed up I would have put him into something loud and ugly but his current garb was very tasteful and downplayed his size instead of accentuating it.

At last he released his firm grip around my waist and held out my chair, which I gladly took.

"White said you'd be here, and here you are." I sensed nervousness from the hulking man in front of me.

"Yes, here I am." I was obviously uncomfortable as well.

"I'm sorry to do this to you, Alex, but I knew this was the only way I'd get a date." All signs of his usual brashness had evaporated, along with his usual manner of speech. "I... Have you looked at the menu yet?" He picked his up from the table and began to study it intently.

"No, not yet. I've never been here. Could you recommend something?"

"Oh, yes." His smile was genuine and grateful as he opened his menu.

As we discussed the menu the awkwardness fell away and the topics of conversation became varied. It didn't take me long to grasp that the person I knew as Helix was nonexistent, he was an invention. An invention to make his clientele more comfortable; make them believe he was just one of them. According to Helix, a big black man needed to walk the walk and talk the talk. It was expected.

When our meals Helix beamed as I complimented him on his choice. The night was full of surprises for me. Not only did Helix's appearance give me a jolt, his taste in food and conversation skills made me happy I'd been tricked into this date. At some point I started considering the whole thing as a date and not a job. I was genuinely sorry the evening was over when Helix made mention of me getting home safely.

We stood at the curb, waiting for my ride to arrive and when it finally did, he handed me his business card. I flipped it over and saw the words *Home Number* and a ten-digit number written on the back. Helix opened the passenger door of the Mustang and nodded a greeting to White. Before I got in, he thanked me for a wonderful evening.

"I had a very nice time too," I replied and stood on my tiptoes to give him a small peck on the cheek before I got in next to White.

"You really shouldn't lead him on like that," White's voice crept into my consciousness.

"What? I had a nice time."

"So, are you going to accept when he calls for another date?" He asked.

"No."

"Because when you give a man a kiss, no matter how innocent, it's an invitation," he interrupted.

"He's quite the gentleman. I just wanted him to know I had a good time." White was starting to piss me off.

Who did White think he was?

He acted as if he were the boss of me. Well, he was my boss, but not the boss of my private life. Well, he kind of was the boss of my private life, too. But, I didn't think I'd led Helix on.

The memory of White and I on the yacht spilled over into my mind. My face flushed and I pulled my bottom lip between my teeth. My heart quickened and I held my breath. The sudden recollection made me feel guilty and I sat quietly.

White's voice jolted me back. "You should be sure of your intentions before you go around kissing random men."

White's vehemence was like a slap to the face.

"Whatever. I'll kiss whomever I feel like kissing." I crossed my arms in front of myself and pushed back into the seat.

Whatever. I didn't set up this stupid date in the first place.

I was out of the car as soon as it came to a stop in the parking garage and started walking toward the lobby.

"Ms. Grey. Wait up."

I did as I was instructed and watched as he made his way across the garage toward me. Then he stuck out his hand, "The card, please."

I'd entirely forgotten about it but handed it to him without hesitation. White snatched the card and immediately left me standing alone. I considered trying to catch up to him, but he seemed to be purposefully walking away from me. I waited the few seconds it took him to enter the lobby before I followed.

White had been grouchy with me before, but never angry. Come to think of it, he was always in charge of his emotions. I'd seen him simulate anger to keep the troops in line or even one of our partners, but I'd never seen him sulk or stomp like a child, until now.

Shift change had occurred because Phil was no longer at his station. Instead, a younger recruit for White and Associates stood in his place. I watched as he tried to greet White but White stormed past. The recruit looked at me with a puzzled look so I gave him a smile and just shrugged. Between the short distance of the garage and lobby I let go of most of my anger with White and embraced my triumphant grin.

I waited for White to enter the elevator by himself and took the next car to my apartment. I considered following him to talk this through, but if he was going to act like a child he could go to his room by himself.

By the time I reached my floor the guilt for kissing Helix ate at me. Even if the kiss had only been on the cheek I hadn't wanted to do anything but thank him for a nice evening. Maybe Black had been right about flaunting my womanhood. However, I reminded myself, even if I had flaunted it, I was told to dress for a date. But, how did I fix this now? I did have a great time with Helix and wouldn't mind getting together with him again. But, I knew I didn't have any feelings for him, other than friendly feelings. I suppose White was right. What if Helix did call for another date? Was a little peck like that really leading him on? I certainly didn't lead White on. As far as I was concerned, I belonged to him. I hoped he realized that.

It never failed. Whenever I thought I knew where I stood with him something changed.

I tossed and turned all night with these thoughts rolling around the bed with me.

Chapter Eight

I WAS UP BEFORE THE SUN and started coffee brewing before Black made his appearance. I knew what I had to do, especially if what White said was true. The last thing I needed was a monstrous man chasing me around town.

Black arrived shortly after the coffee was done and we sat in silence for two cups apiece before he finally asked me if I were ready.

The drive to the gym didn't take long enough. I didn't know what to expect from Helix or exactly what to say to him so I hesitated when Black held the door open for me.

"Let's go," he hiked his head toward the door.

Black got his point across with as few words as possible and I was compelled to walk inside.

Helix came out of his office as we walked in. He and Black greeted each other in their usual manner of grabbing the other's forearm in a shake that would tear anyone else's arm off.

"Long time," Helix said as he eyeballed me in the expected manner I was uncomfortable with.

"Lookin' good," he added with a wag of his eyebrows. The toothy grin dropped away and his tone became more civilized. "Can we talk a moment?"

Being met, in this environment, with the man I'd gone out on a date with last night, jolted me.

"Of course." I looked at Black for encouragement and was rewarded with a slight smile that seemed to suggest he knew exactly what was going on and he enjoyed every second of it.

I stepped into Helix's office and he shut the door.

I'm trapped.

I didn't know if he'd try anything or not, but I hoped he didn't push it too far. I wasn't sure I could fight him off if I had to.

"I'm glad you showed up today," he said.

My unease lessened as he looked at his feet. I expected him to kick the dirt across the floor instead of try to kiss me.

After a short pause he continued, "I don't think you and I are right for each other." He immediately added, "I didn't feel any... there was no... well, it was obvious you didn't have sex on your mind."

"I did have a great time," I didn't know what else to say. I'd really thought White was right and I'd have to fight Helix off.

"Me too." He squared his shoulder and regained a wolfish grin. "Next time I have info I'll request to deliver it to you. We'll go out and paint the town red or whatever other color we feel like paintin' it. It's nice to have a sexy bi... chick on your arm." With this last statement he put out his arm for me to take and led me back to the waiting Black.

The two men nodded some sort of understanding between them when Helix and I exited his office.

While Black and I sparred my mind wandered. Black hadn't said a thing about the date with Helix but it was obvious he knew about it. When we finally took a break I asked him how he knew I'd gone out on a date with Helix.

"He brought it up to me first."

"You told him I'd be interested?" I was shocked.

"No, I told him you'd probably go, as a job."

I was okay with that. Black *was* right. I probably would have gone, even if I had known it was Helix I was meeting.

"You're right." I dodged his fist. "Why didn't he just ask me?"

Black barked a single, "Ha."

He lunged at me and again I dodged.

"What's funny?"

"It was his way of testing the waters at the office."

"What?" It was my turn to attack unsuccessfully.

"You weren't the resistance he was the most worried about." Black smirked as if he had a secret.

I stopped sparring.

"You're saying he did this to find out if I was dating anyone inside the company?"

Black hadn't dropped his fighting stance and moved toward me. His smirk grew and his eyebrows went up for emphasis.

"So?" I side-stepped his charge at the last second and didn't take the opportunity to give his kidneys a quick jab.

"So, what?" He must have realized I was taking a break because he stopped his next advance.

"Did I pass the test?"

"Did he ask you out again?"

I shook my head.

"Then I'd say, no."

I didn't know if this was a good thing or not. Of course I didn't want Helix to be pining for me, but I didn't want him to think I was involved with anyone inside the company. There was nothing I could do about it now so I squared off with Black again.

"Why didn't White tell me who I was meeting with before I got there?"

"You know White. He likes the covert ops so he tries to make everything covert. Besides, Helix asked that you not be told. He figured his chances were better if you didn't know who you were meeting." He shrugged. "Got everything worked out?" He indicated Helix with a jerk of his head.

"Yeah." I sighed.

Black raised his eyebrows.

"I didn't know Helix was so—"

"Different?" Black supplied.

"Yeah, I wish I was attracted to him. We could have some fun." I stepped back from Black. "Do you have a deal with Red? He always tries to get me to talk about this kind of thing."

"Nope, no deal with Red. You offered," he smiled his rare smile. "Now, if you'll excuse me, I have a little business of my own."

He left me standing alone beside the mat as he walked into Helix's office. I looked around for somewhere to go to get out of the way. Gray and orange plastic chairs lined the wall near the front door that looked like they'd held more than their fair share of weight. It was the only place to sit, so I gathered our stuff and made myself as comfortable as I could.

I watched the men and the women spar and beat up on the other available punching bags without faces. I silently critiqued them and thought I might make a good instructor for self-defense classes. Though I knew I would never do it, I found myself daydreaming about owning my own gym. Helix intruded into my dream. My mind had made him my partner, in more than just the gym. He called me Honey, but in White's voice. This made me sit straight up in my seat and look around guiltily.

I changed my thoughts to what Black might be talking about with Helix. What kind of informant or operative was Helix and was his name Helix or Johnson or Helix Johnson?

The two mountainous men walked out of Helix's office before I could wipe the smile from my face.

"Ready?" was all that Black said as he reached down for his pack.

"See ya soon, baby." Helix's goodbye boomed across the gym as we walked out. I wasn't at all uncomfortable with him anymore.

"So?" I asked as soon as Black was in the driver's seat of his SUV.

"So?" he repeated.

"So, what was your business?" I spelled it out, though we both knew what I was talking about.

"The same old."

"Just tell me. It's not like I'm going to tell anyone else." The secrecy in the company was something I was getting tired of. "If you don't tell me, I'll just find out on my own anyway,"

"Probably not. But, if you find out on your own, I'm not to blame for telling you."

I rolled my eyes and let out a groan.

This brought a reciprocal sigh from Black and he gave me some more information. He told me Helix didn't just own a gym. He dealt in black market weapons.

"He's your friend." My mouth hung open mirroring my wide eyes.

A recent job for White and Associates, and Penumbra, had been to deal with black market weapons dealers. Penumbra had shot and killed at least six men in less than two minutes because of a deal like that.

"Helix is a bit of a gray hat. He works *for* the government but actually lives the life. He's allowed to make some money under the table as long as the proper authorities are informed as to where the weapons are and who has them. It's part of his job to inform about the big-ticket items like RPG's and large shipments of automatic rifles and such. This is priceless information. He's actively watching specific individuals and companies as well."

I understood everything Black had said but, "Gray hat?" This term had me confused.

"You know. White hats and black hats?"

When I didn't respond, Black continued to explain. "White hats, good guys? Black hats, bad guys?"

"Oh." Helix was living between good and bad.

Black talked a little more about Helix's role. He was the middleman. He was the man with the connections. The information about Johns' and Grigori's meeting in Alaska, the little party that Penumbra killed, could easily have come from him. He reported directly to the government but sometimes worked with our company.

We sat in silence the remainder of the ride to the office. Me, thinking about Helix and his gray hat association and Black thinking about absolutely nothing as far as I could tell.

When we reached the 7th floor I wanted to follow Black into the office to hear what intelligence he'd gleaned from Helix but I knew I wasn't invited so I remained on the elevator. I needed a shower anyway.

As soon as I was clean I took a stormy trip back down to the office. My infatuation with White had clouded my vision of the bigger picture. I'd been too busy thinking about White's reaction to the innocent kiss I'd given Helix. The fact that I'd actually been pimped out hadn't even dawned on me until now.

All the important information was being discussed without me, yet I was being prostituted. I was angry that White would do that and then have the audacity to act possessive. My company and my affections were not for sale. I planned to tell him so.

Gabriella smiled as I walked in but quickly dropped the smile when I didn't return the happy sentiment. She cocked her head toward the intercom and I shook my head no in response. I was going to fulfill her need for entertainment. She always loved it when I barged in.

I strode across the room and right into White's office.

"So, how'd it go with Helix this morning?" White asked before I started in on him.

"Great. He interpreted the kiss on the cheek exactly how it was meant. I guess some men can tell the difference," I jabbed back.

"Lucky for you. Helix isn't the kind you want to get involved with. Not with the job you have now. The life he lives, it's highly possible you two would clash." He meant Penumbra.

"Well, if I were more informed—"

"I had no idea you'd ever consider kissing *Helix* ." His voice went up an octave and his chair rolled away as he stood.

"It was spur of the moment. He was such a gentleman and we actually have a lot in common." I didn't let my voice gain any volume but I had no objections to the venom that dropped from my words.

I wanted to slap White for being such a jerk and then I wanted to slap myself for caring enough to get mad.

"Yeah, Alex. He's a player. He knows how to turn on the charm for whatever type it is he's going for next. The man's been undercover for years and knows how to play the part. He certainly didn't miss his mark this time." White took his seat again with a heavy sigh.

"Spoken by another player. Not like any of his secrets are secrets to you. Well, excuse me for enjoying myself on a job. And I'm sorry I'm so naïve. Maybe I'll just whore out and get some experience."

I couldn't believe I'd just said that. I felt my face heat up and White's expression was one of pure glee. This succeeded in fueling the flames.

"It's not funny!"

"Whore out? I haven't ever heard it put that way before. That's hilarious." He stood from his desk and his expression changed again.

"Don't you dare!" I backed away. "I'm not pleased with you at the moment and I haven't been for a few days now. I don't appreciate being forced into a dark room and told not to try to get out."

White opened his mouth to speak, but I held up my finger in warning.

"And, having the man I've just trusted with everything, and I mean *everything*, pimp me out to another man, is more than insulting."

White didn't say a word and his look was not undecipherable for once. He actually looked ashamed of himself. There was some surprise evident on his face as well, as if he'd never considered he'd been pandering for another man.

"I promised I wouldn't pry, so I won't." I continued. "But, if you don't find something for me to do I'm going to go straight to my dad or even Colin for Penumbra jobs or anything else I can get."

"I'm your handler," he argued.

"I'm not kidding, Rick. I understand that there are things that go along with this job that I might not always like. I'm even willing to deal with the *need-to-know* crap, for the most part. But, I'm done playing the part of escort and I'm done sitting on my ass. With the exception of our latest yachting adventure, it's been months since I've done anything outside of this building. If you don't have anything for me, fine. Just know that I *will* find something to do."

"I'll get something set up, I promise. And, for what it's worth, I'm sorry for the Helix thing." His face was somber.

"Whatever."

I knew I'd forgive him, I was already more than half way there, but I wasn't ready to admit it. He could worry for a while.

His shoulders were slack and his step was hesitant, but I knew what he was doing. He was on his way over to *make up* with me.

"Not going to happen." I shook my head and turned to leave.

"I really am sorry, Alex." His voice was miserable. For some reason, this made me hold my chin up with more conviction.

I didn't respond and shut his office door with a little extra force.

"What's going on?" Gabriella asked as soon as the sound of the door slamming shut faded.

"Nothing important. I've about had all I can stand of this office building."

"Well, call me if you need anything, Hon," she said as I turned to walk out of the office.

"Thanks, Gabriella."

Chapter Nine

I HADN'T BEEN BACK TO MY apartment for fifteen minutes before a knock came on my door.

"Lets go," Black said as soon as I opened the door.

I didn't hesitate and stepped from my apartment and followed him onto the elevator and down to his SUV. I didn't question him until we reached the airport.

"Where are we going?" I had nothing but the clothes on my back and we were about to hop on a plane.

"Survival training."

"Haven't I already done that?"

"Not quite." We didn't talk again for the entire flight.

We landed at the Wyoming compound later that day. Situated in a green clearing and surrounded by trees and mountains, the compound was impressive. From the air I could see groups of men scattered across the compound involved in various activities. I remembered the lax feel of the Alaskan compound and that vibe was definitely missing here. As soon as we landed a recruit pulled along side the plane in a Jeep and waited for us. A cursory glimpse into one of the hangers, as I stepped into the Jeep, showed me that the hanger bays were also full of men in greasy coveralls attending different aircraft and vehicles.

The officer's quarters, like at the other compounds, were on the second floor.

"I'll be over in a bit," Black said and went down the corridor to his own room.

I stepped into a small apartment with an open floor plan. It felt familiar and comfortable. The only door, other than the exit, led to the bathroom. There was a small dining area, a small kitchenette to the left of the dining area, and a full sized bed sat back in its own small cubby with a couple of dressers.

Within seconds of walking into my room a light tapping had me back at the door. A young man stood on the other side with his arms full of items.

I stepped aside and let him walk past me. He walked to the small dining table and poured the goods out of his arms.

A bottle of shampoo almost rolled to the floor, but he caught it just in time.

"Commander Grey." He addressed me with a salute as soon as his hands were free.

"Hi." I smiled.

I didn't know if I should address him as cadet, recruit or some other title. Saluting and ranks just weren't my thing and I didn't care for either. I could understand the need for rank when it came to missions. Someone had to be in charge. But, the system had always confused me. The same went for saluting. I knew there was a correct way to salute and several incorrect ways. I'd spent more time in front of my mirror practicing sticking my legs out of various dresses than I had saluting. Actually, I'd never spent any time in front of the mirror to practice my salute.

The poor guy stood for a full twenty seconds with his hand at his brow before he gave up.

"Ma'am." He turned toward the table. "These are for your stay."

He lifted a pair of bath towels, wash cloths and hand towels, then retrieved the shampoo he'd saved, a bottle of conditioner and a bar of soap still in its box and laid them on top of the towels in his arms. He stood still, holding the pile.

I reached out awkwardly with both hands, intending to take the items from him.

He pulled them closer to his body and said, "I'll take care of it, Ma'am."

He turned on his heels and carried it all to the bathroom.

I took the opportunity to start rummaging through what remained in the pile on the table. There were three changes of clothes and a pair of boots in my size. I took one set of clothes and laid them out on the bed and put the remaining clothes in the drawers. The man was standing stiffly behind me when I turned around.

"The refrigerator isn't stocked. I apologize."

"That's okay."

The two of us stood staring at each other for several seconds.

"Thanks." I finally said.

"Of course, Ma'am."

He remained.

"You aren't getting a tip. I left all my cash at home."

This brought a flash of a smile to his face and his voice was a bit lighter when he asked, "Is there anything else I can do for you, ma'am?"

"Oh!" I caught on. "You are dismissed," I said as if I'd just accomplished something.

He smiled briefly and looked me in the eye. "If you need anything else, please ask for Cadet Clemment."

As soon as the door shut behind him I changed into the clothes waiting on my bed. Black was at my door before I finished lacing up my boots carrying a stack of clothes.

"I already got my clothes." I pointed to the bundle in his arms.

"Good. Bring them."

I went directly to the drawers and pulled out my extra clothes and set them on the table while I bent down to finish lacing my boot and Black sat across from me.

"Hurry up with those laces. We're leaving in about an hour and we still have to gear up and address the men."

"The men?" I picked up my pace. "We aren't going out alone?"

"No. We're teaching the class."

This was new. "I've never taught survival training before." I didn't know what was expected of me.

"Just follow my lead. Ready?"

I picked up my clothes and followed him out of Headquarters to the equipment building. There were ten men milling around the building when we walked up. When they noticed us they fell into formation.

Black walked past them as if they weren't even there. He held the door open for me and entered the building behind me.

"Are the packs ready?" He asked the recruit behind the desk.

I assumed they were since there was a nice straight line of twelve packs against the wall.

"Yes, sir." He had also stood at attention.

"Which ones are mine and Commander Grey's?"

The man stepped from behind the desk and grabbed up two packs and hauled them back to the desk.

Black immediately inspected the contents of his pack, so I did the same. It had a couple canteens, some Meals

Ready-to-Eat, or better known as MREs, the standard issue knife that had come in so handy for me at other times, and a multi-tool with a shovel.

"That's called an E-Tool," Black said when I held it up. "It's an entrenching tool, but it's good for lots of things."

There were several other items, including a nice pair of binoculars, that I put back and then shoved my clothes on top of it all.

"I'll send the men in for their packs," Black told the recruit.

"Yes, sir," he barked.

When we stepped out of the building it looked as if the men hadn't moved a muscle since we went in. It was impressive to see a line of fit men, willing to do whatever we told them. Black walked in front of them and looked them up and down.

"Packs!" he yelled at them and pointed to the building.

They hustled, single file, into the building. In less than two minutes the assembly line was complete and the line of men was adorned with packs.

"Fall in!" He commanded. The men obeyed without question and we began a hard jog toward the tree line.

We kept up this pace until it became too dark to see clearly. Black stopped near another small clearing that was barely big enough to hold all twelve of us. The men walked around in circles, huffing. Some held their sides and both Black and I were out of breath as well. Black and I opened our canteens and took long swigs.

In a low voice Black told me, "We'll stay here for the night. Keep close to me tonight." I gave him a strange look I didn't know if he could see in the low light and he added, "You and I will leave early in the morning and I don't want to disturb the men to come find you." It was only then that I realized there were no bedrolls with our packs. It was going to be an unpleasant night.

"Pick a spot, men. The work starts tomorrow," Black said with no hint he'd been out of breath at all.

The two of us sat down by the nearest tree. The men followed our example. I used my pack as a pillow and fell asleep right away. The first time I woke up it was because of some rustling off in the trees. The moon had risen and there was some light to see by. The rustling sound came nearer and I watched as one of the men came back into the clearing and lay back down on the ground.

My next waking moment was because a stick had, somehow, crawled under me and was trying to meld to my hipbone. I removed the offending stick and did a quick head count. When I was satisfied I went back to sleep.

Over the course of the next few hours I was in and out of sleep as my shivers woke me. Eventually, I gave in and rummaged through my pack for my survival blanket. It was folded up into a tiny square and made considerable noise as I unwrapped it. I didn't care. Black already looked comfortable inside his own blanket. How he'd done it so quietly was something I'd have to ask him later.

I didn't wake up again until 4:00 AM, but this time, I folded my blanket back up as quietly and small as I could and put it back into my pack. I looked around at the men strewn across the ground and noticed some had their blankets over them but the rest were huddled together or in fetal positions.

"Morning." Black whispered from behind me. He sounded subdued and a little tired.

I turned to face him. "Morning," I replied. "Wish we had some coffee," I whispered as I rubbed my hands together to warm them up.

"Me too." He looked around at the men then hiked his head off to the side. "Lets go." We grabbed up our packs and hiked away from the men for several minutes. The moon still lit our way, so the going was easy.

When we stopped he pulled out a penlight and a map. "The men are here and *our* destination is—" he slid the light over the map a considerable distance, "here." It would probably take us at least two days of hard hiking to make it, if the terrain was favorable and according to the map, it was anything but.

"Okay?"

"The catch." Black looked at me, "The men will be hunting us. They each have a briefing packet in their packs. It's just a matter of time before one of them finds it. They've done these kinds of drills before so, the odds are they'll be hunting us before too long. They don't have our rendezvous point, so they will have to track us. We are not allowed to do anything but evade, but," he lifted the light back up to the map, "you see this spot?" He highlighted what looked like a ranger tower.

I nodded.

"This is a cache of training weapons. If they're smart, that's the first place they will head and someplace we should completely avoid."

"Understood," I said.

"But," he added, "There's a radio at that location that we need to retrieve. We can't complete our mission without it."

"Of course," I said.

"So, that is the first place we need to go, as well. Speed is the most important part right now, since we know where they will be going and it doesn't matter if they find traces of us on the way. We just have to stay at least one step ahead of them before we get to the cache. Then we need to be miles away. Let's get moving. I'll explain in more detail on the way there."

We started out at a hard run and kept this up for an hour. The moonlight was strong enough that we were able to avoid almost all hazards. We each stumbled a couple of times, but managed to keep our feet and our pace. By the time the sun started to light the sky we were comfortable enough with our small lead to walk for a bit. Black took this time to finish briefing me.

The cache of weapons sounded really cool. According to Black, the clothes we all wore had micro sensors in them that would detect a hit as if a real bullet had been fired at us. Of course, this all relied on laser technology, and the sensors were a little more sensitive and faster than a real bullet. So, essentially, if we made it into their sites, and they pulled the trigger, it was game over. An alarm, located in our packs would go off and we were supposed to sit and wait for the team to retrieve us. It also had its drawbacks. If the shooter didn't have a clear line of sight, the laser wouldn't reach us. Something as simple as a leaf could get in the way.

Black told me, "If one of us gets shot, the other needs to get the hell out of there. We still win if one of us completes the mission."

Then he went on to explain when we reached our destination we would find a strong box with our very own set of weapons and a code in it that we needed to radio in. Once we did that, the tables turned.

"As soon as they get that order, they will set their sites on their new destination." He continued to tell me that they wouldn't be as limited as we were because they were allowed to use their weapons for defense while trying to reach their rendezvous point.

"I'd like to do this as a team, but if you'd rather split up, we can."

"Teamwork sounds good to me."

"Good." We moved into a hard jog and made good progress for the rest of the day. It was late afternoon when we reached the cache. If we were lucky, we had at least an hour on the men and maybe more. Two people could move faster than ten.

We entered another small clearing that held a wooden and rickety-looking tower.

"Up there." Black pointed.

I didn't hesitate and started climbing the ladder. Once I reached the top I went directly to the green metal box I spotted in the far corner. When I opened it, I found several different weapons. Ten pistols, eight automatic rifles, and two sniper rifles. My fingers itched but I only grabbed one of the radios lying on the top of the stash.

I took a second to rummage around in my pack for my binoculars. If I could find out how close or far the men were, it would be helpful, and this was a great vantage point.

It didn't take me long to find them and they were maybe thirty minutes away if they were moving at our pace. I hurriedly stowed the binoculars and radio in my pack and slid down the ladder.

"About thirty minutes hike that way." I indicated the direction we'd just come from with my head.

"Lets move," was all Black said and I fell in line behind him.

I hoped it would take the men longer to distribute their weapons than it took us to grab our radio.

After fifteen minutes of hard moving, Black slowed and said we needed to start moving more carefully, covering our tracks. Chances are the men would approach the cache with caution. They didn't know we were given orders not to engage. That would give us a little more time to get a little farther ahead. And, we needed to be cautious after they gained the tower with their own binoculars and sniper rifles.

"We need to get to higher ground," I told him as we took care to cover our tracks.

"Good idea." He stopped and took his map out of his pack. "Here it is. We aren't far." He pointed to a ridge on the map. "We might have to do some free climbing. You up to it?"

Free climbing was dangerous, but, "Hell yeah," I said and we altered our course slightly.

Within half an hour we were at the base of a sheer cliff. Both of us looked up and opted to search for a different starting point with better handholds and a better angle. We walked carefully along the base for five minutes, but finally I saw a good spot.

It would be dark in a few hours and I was tired. But, we couldn't rest if we wanted to make it through the night. I was sure we weren't the only ones with the cool binoculars. When night fell we'd have to be out of sight and have a significant lead.

"What do you think? We're starting to lose the light." I said, pointing up.

Black looked up from putting back a rock he'd overturned. "You're the faster climber. Get up there and tie off a rope. I can climb the rope pretty quickly."

"Here." I handed him my pack after I fished out a rope and slung it over my shoulder. "You think we have time to haul it up? I'll move a lot faster without it."

"Probably, if we hurry. If not, I'll try to carry them both up."

"Think the rope is long enough?" I asked as I started to climb.

"Standard issue is a hundred foot rope. Looks like sixty feet to the top. Should be enough."

"I hope so."

We quit talking and I made excellent time, considering I was free climbing. I decided that it was best that I'd gone first. My hands and feet fit into more places than Black's would and I wasn't as cautious as he was. When I reached the top I couldn't help but knock some dirt loose. I just hoped it wouldn't be obvious enough to let the men know we were on top of the ridge.

When I reached the top of the cliff I realized I still wasn't at the top of the hill. After a short distance of fairly level footing the ground continued up several more feet before it crested. I went straight to the closest tree with a large enough diameter to hold Black's weight, tied off the rope and threw it down to Black. When I turned around I got a great view of the tower off in the distance.

"Shit," I said and dropped to the ground. I crawled to the edge and said to Black in as quiet a voice as possible, "I can see the tower from here." He put his fingers to his eyes and pointed in the direction of the tower, meaning I should scope it out. I threw the rope down and pointed at my pack at his feet. He quickly tied it to the rope and I hauled it up as fast as I could.

I backed away and took cover near some thicker bushes and trees near the edge and dug out my binoculars. The tower was empty and so was the small clearing so I moved my search in a little closer to our location and still didn't find them. I scanned the clearing and tower to find the same thing, nothing. I broadened my search and I finally thought I saw some movement on the edge of the clearing. When I was sure it was them I told Black, "Hurry and get your ass up here. They don't have their weapons yet."

I heard a little whistle so I tore my eyes away from the troop of men filing into the clearing long enough to look down at Black.

"Rope," he said.

"Shit." I swore again and quickly untied my pack and tossed down the rope. As soon as I let go of the rope I put the binoculars back to my eyes and watched two of them carefully approach the tower. The rest of the men held back on the edge of the clearing. One of the men climbed the tower ladder and my stomach jumped into my throat. I glanced at Black's progress.

"Hurry," I hissed.

He was within five feet of the top. I heard an angry grunt and the sound of dirt and rocks hitting the ground below. My eyes were glued to the men as the first one reached the top of the tower. The rest of the men around the clearing had slowly started making their way toward the center of the clearing and they made a quick sprint when the one inside the tower gave the all clear.

By this time, Black joined me at the ledge.

"You made good time." I moved behind the tree the rope was tied to.

"The hardest part is always getting over the edge." He rolled over on his back and took in some deep breaths.

The rope untied, I made a nice coil as I pulled it to me. Black joined me so I nudged the binoculars I'd laid at my feet.

"Keep an eye out, will ya?"

"Yes, ma'am." He retrieved the binoculars and brought them to his face as he leaned around the tree.

"They're still distributing the weapons. You done with that rope yet? We have to get to the other side of this ridge."

"Good enough." I put the coil of rope over my shoulder and sprinted for the top of the hill.

Black was right behind me with both packs. We crested the hill in a matter of seconds. The other side was steeper than I anticipated and my feet slipped out from under me. I hit the ground hard and slid a few feet.

"You okay?" Black asked when I stopped sliding.

"Yeah," I groaned.

I rolled over and saw him lying on his stomach peering over the edge of the hill with my binoculars, our packs beside him. I climbed back up to the top.

"Going to be a challenge to hide my slide down the hill," I complained quietly.

"I doubt they'll find it any time soon. Looks like they're setting up camp. It's a good defensible position and they can see a lot from the tower, if they keep watch. We'll have to stay on the far side of this ridge for now."

He handed me my binoculars and I scanned the tower area. He was right. They were setting up camp, all except two of them. They were scouting on ahead and I could see they followed our trail.

"We've got scouts." I handed him the binoculars and he took a look.

"Better get going, then," he said as he stuffed the binoculars back into my pack. "Stay low." He slid down the hill on his butt.

Chapter Ten

WE HIKED STEADILY UNTIL DARKNESS fell. Then we sat down, each with our backs to the same tree. Neither of us removed our packs. Instead, we used them, as well as the tree, for a backrest.

"Take a nap. I'll keep watch for the first hour, then I'll get a little rest and we can head out again when the moon comes up."

I followed my orders and woke up to Black's deep voice near my face. "Up. Quietly."

The moon hadn't risen yet and I could barely see Black in the darkness, but I could hear some rustling in the distance. Black and I moved to the opposite side of the tree from the noise. He quietly unzipped my pack that was still on my back and took out my binoculars. He switched on the night vision mode and did a sweep.

I stayed as close to the tree as possible until he said, "Think it's a moose."

He handed me the binoculars. When I put them to my eyes I realized he'd switched over to infrared at some point and I could clearly see a moose nearby.

Black had already sat back down on the ground near my feet, so I joined him.

"Yep. Moose." I sighed.

"Get some more sleep," he said.

"No. You take your turn. I'm not going to be able to sleep again for a while. I'll wake you when it gets brighter."

"You sure?" he asked.

"Positive."

The moose stayed nearby for quite some time and I kept jumping at the sounds and scanning the area with my binoculars. Finally, the moon lit up the sky and I gently nudged Black awake.

"The moose is gone and it's been pretty quiet for a while now. You want to head out?"

"We better get some more distance between us and them. I suspect if the scouts were able to track us after we started covering our tracks they didn't come any nearer than the cliff face. It was getting dark and that was a hell of a climb with good light. According to the map, the cliff extends at least a mile north of where we ascended. If the scouts are following protocol, they won't stray too far from the rest of the men."

He turned his back to me. "Get the map from my pack."

He cupped his light so it wouldn't be so noticeable as he did a quick scan of the map.

"If we follow this little valley we're already in, and move hard, we might be able to make the rendezvous spot by tomorrow. But, that means we'll leave an easy trail for them to track." He waited for my input.

"With us not having any weapons, I think our best bet is to haul ass to the cache. If we move fast, we should definitely be able to stay in front of them." I said. "I worry about those two sniper rifles more than anything else, but I think our only chance is to get our weapons and *then* get under cover. After we have our weapons, as long as I find a sniper rifle," I mused, "we can ambush them when they hit the clearing."

"We have to call in the code before we can take the offensive." Black's voice startled me a bit.

"I don't see how that's a problem. We'll call it in after they're already in range. Then, with our end fulfilled we can take the offensive. If we have at least one sniper rifle I should be able to take out at least five of them before they know what hit 'em, maybe more with the laser sight since it has a faster reaction time than bullets." I'd slipped deep into my thoughts. "If we can just get to the cache at least half an hour before they do, that should give me enough time to find a good location—" I grinned as I watched it unfold in my mind.

"You sound pretty confident." Black's voice brought me back to reality.

"Do you think there will be a sniper rifle in the cache?"
I asked.

"Yes. We each get a pistol and then we'll get our choice
of rifles, but we can only take one each. You sure you want to
lug a sniper rifle as we chase after them?"

"Yeah. I'm best with the sniper rifle."

"Sounds good. Lets get a move on. You take the lead."

I set out with a purpose. There was a sniper rifle out there
with my name on it and I was determined to get to it as
quickly as possible.

I pushed on until late morning before Black called a
temporary halt so we could eat and get some fluids down.
I finished my MRE as fast as I could and not just because I
couldn't stand the taste. I knew we didn't have much chance
of making it out of here *alive* until we had weapons and
permission to defend ourselves.

Black climbed to a higher spot for a better view.

"No signs," he said when he rejoined me.

"I hate not knowing where they are," I complained.

"Me too."

"We better get back to it." We each took another swig
from our canteens and then headed out again.

We stopped periodically, so Black could sweep the area
for any signs of our pursuers but by early afternoon we still
hadn't seen any signs of them and we'd found the other
tower with our cache. We approached cautiously. It wasn't
likely, but it was possible the opposing force had guessed our
destination and were lying in wait.

"I'm going to go for it," I told Black after we'd sat on the outskirts of the clearing for five minutes.

"If they take me out, you'll know they are out there and you can get out of here." Then I realized. "There's no winning for us if we don't get this code."

"Nope. If they get you now, we're done."

"Crap," I said.

"Give me your pack." He held out his hand and I complied. Then he said, "Run fast, climb fast and grab that code." With that, he ran out into the clearing carrying my pack and I sprinted out after him. He ran in a zigzag and I did the same. I made the tower in only a few seconds and sprinted up the ladder. If they were going to take me, now would be the time.

I reached the top and my alarm wasn't going off. I flipped open the box and grabbed the code and two pistols and shoved them in my pockets. Then I grabbed up one of the sniper rifles. I called down to Black, "Sniper rifle or automatic?"

"Auto," he called back.

I slung the two rifles over my back. It was awkward climbing back down. The guns wanted to get caught up in my legs. I was thankful I didn't still have my pack on. That would have made the climb down even harder. Ten feet from the ground, Black called out to drop his rifle. He caught it and slung it over his shoulder.

When I reached the ground we each grabbed our own packs, sprinted to the opposite edge of the clearing and took cover behind some trees. I pulled out the code and one of the pistols and handed them to Black.

He pulled out his map and asked me where I wanted to set up. I didn't even glance at the map and pointed off behind us. "I saw a great spot when I was up in the tower. It's not too far that way."

"Did you happen to see any movement when you were up there?"

"No, I didn't. I thought the tower might be a good spot to make our stand. But I think we'll be better off up there. It's a bit of a climb so we better hurry."

"Lead on," he said.

It took us half an hour to reach the locale I'd seen from the tower but once in position I said, "Those towers aren't in the best spots for fire spotting."

"No, they're strictly used for this type of exercise." He pointed off to our left. "There's a real fire tower over there. They put them on the highest peaks so they can see everything." I could barely see it off in the distance.

Black brought his binoculars to his eyes and searched the area while I made myself comfortable in the prone position and started my own search through my scope.

"There," Black said, pointing in the general direction of the tower we'd recently left.

I drew my vision from my scope and followed the line of his finger. He pointed in the general direction of the tower we'd recently left. The men were coming in hard on our trail.

"You're sure about this?" Black asked.

He held the radio near his face and dug in his pocket for the code.

"Yep."

"Let me know when you want me to radio it in." He readied himself in the prone position with the radio and code in one hand, the rifle under the other hand and his eye on his scope.

I watched. The men hesitated on the edge of the clearing trying to find concealment behind the brush. I expected them to send one out to the tower and then follow when they thought it was clear. That's when I'd get them. I'd have to take the tower first. I waited.

The men spread out in a half circle around the clearing with their two snipers on either end of the line and the two scouts were actively searching for our trail. Realizing they were taking up defensive positions around the tower I changed my plan of attack. The man on point was scouring the area with his binoculars. I decided he'd be the first to go because he'd be the one most likely to pinpoint my position after I made my first shot.

"Ready," I told Black.

"Geronimo," he said into the radio.

As soon as he said it, I watched the men scramble and I pulled the trigger. *One... two... three... four... five... six... seven... eight... nine... ten.* I counted in my head as I fired.

The silence of the weapon and the lack of a kick was unnerving. I stared through my scope for a full minute. It wasn't just the silence of the gun that was disconcerting. Black hadn't said anything either.

I pulled my eye from the scope. Black stared at me.

"What?" I asked.

"Nothing. Ready to go?"

"Yep." I stood and waited for him to lead us down the hill. As we hiked down, I worried that I shouldn't have shown him what I was capable of, and was having a hard time reading his silence. Black was normally quiet and to the point, but the look he'd given me kept replaying in my mind.

Descending the hill didn't take nearly as long as going up and we were back at the edge of the clearing within fifteen minutes.

He stopped and said, "That was very impressive, Commander Grey. I didn't pull my trigger once. Have you been practicing?"

"Every chance I get." I didn't lie.

He nodded, raised his eyebrows, and donned a knowing grin. "How about we head back to Headquarters tonight? There's a road to the east of here. It's less than a quarter of a mile away. I could call in for transport."

"Sounds good to me," I said.

Black pulled out his radio and changed the frequency before speaking into it. When he finished, we walked into the clearing together. The men milled about until they caught sight of us, then they fell into ranks and stood at attention. As soon as we stopped they all saluted.

Black and I didn't salute back and Black said, "At ease. The mission is completed. Our rides will be here shortly. Lets get to the road and get home."

A resounding "Yes, sir!" from the men set us in motion toward the road.

We were all back at Headquarters within the hour. After we'd filed out of the vehicles, Black addressed the group.

"Good job, men. Too bad you couldn't win." He paced in front of them. "There will be *no* discussion about this training op between you until all of the testing is complete. Is this clear?" He wasn't yelling, but his tone made me cringe.

"Yes, sir!" they said in unison.

"Dismissed!" He yelled.

The salute they gave made Black's brow furrow and he looked at me accusingly.

"Who the hell keeps telling them to salute?"

"Not me," I said with a grin.

"We need to talk." He marched into the building and straight to my room.

I sat at the table and waited for him to start talking.

"You aren't going to make us some coffee?"

I shuffled out of my chair and rummaged through the kitchenette until I found the coffee and started a pot brewing.

"There." I regained my seat. "What did you want to talk about?"

"I'd only planned on the one time out, but we're here and have the time. Do you want to do it again?" He asked.

"Sure." I shrugged.

"It's a little unfair to the other recruits, since we've already run the course, but," he smiled, "I had *fun* ."

"I missed the trees." I sighed.

"I missed it all." He added and the two of us sat quietly until the coffee was brewed. I got up and retrieved us each a cup and we savored our first couple of sips.

"I didn't think you'd done anything like this before."

"I haven't," I lied.

While we finished our coffee he made a couple calls to set up our next excursion.

"Get some rest. We'll leave first thing in the morning."

WE CYCLED THROUGH THREE MORE teams of ten with the exact same outcome. Not one team was able to out maneuver us at the last clearing. Even though the end result was the same, each run was unique. We decided to leave a clear path for all of the men to follow so they'd be close on our heels and we wouldn't have to wait too long for them to get to the last tower before we picked them off. One of the teams sent a single man to the tower to do some scouting before they came at us. If only the outfits we wore would have allowed for some camo we wouldn't have been located. All the same, we took them out as they crossed the clearing to get to us.

With the fourth exercise complete, Black and I sat in my room at Headquarters, sipping our ritual *after mission* cup of coffee. Four pots wouldn't alleviate my exhaustion. A full night in a real bed is what I needed.

"What would you say to switching it up a bit?" he asked.

"What do you have in mind?"

"You didn't need me out there. You seem to work better alone."

"You want me to do the next one alone?"

"Not quite." His eyes narrowed.

"What then?" His expression made me more than a little nervous. What did he have planned?

"I'll give you a full day head start."

"Just you and me?"

"No. Just you and us."

"You mean the entire compound?" I was flabbergasted.

"No, just the men that we've taken through once before."

"Are you nuts? That's forty men. I'd never make it back."

"Forty-one," He pointed to his own chest. "And, I'm not so sure. You've already taken them all out once before. Did you realize I didn't pull my trigger once? I specifically didn't even try after our first outing."

"What? You didn't even try to help me?" I put my hands on my hips.

"When you took ten men out in less than ten seconds, I was curious. You even went through the motions of pulling back the bolt with each shot as if you were really taking the shot. You could've taken them even faster had you just pulled the trigger, like the gun allows."

"Were you trying to get me killed out there? We were supposed to be a team."

"We were never acting as a team, I was just a weight around your neck each time out. I watched you. You could have done it alone, and done it better."

Was this a veiled accusation?

"I'm a team player."

"I know that, and that's why I never got shot. I'm not saying you're not a team player. What I'm saying is that I think we found your true calling. You're a hunter. You didn't hesitate, you didn't flinch, you didn't stop."

I sat quietly. If I could have a full day head start I could probably make a nice dent in his troop.

"Think of it as an experiment." Black interrupted my thoughts.

"*Your* experiment." I added.

"Yes. Mine. I can't help it. I'm curious. I think you could take out more than half of us before we get you."

Why am I even considering this?

I couldn't take them all at once. I might have gotten them all in groups of ten, but this was forty men *and* Black. Yet, the temptation to try was strong. I kept replaying possible scenarios through my mind.

"Do all of my kills have to be with the rifle or pistol?"

"No. If you can get up close and personal and inflict a killing blow, it'll count. But, only if you promise to be careful. I don't need any training accidents on my hands."

"Are we talking twenty-four hours or twelve hours as a full day?"

"Probably sixteen hours. Normal waking hours."

"It's going to be really hard without any real camo."

"So? Tomorrow?"

"Tomorrow sounds like a good day to die," I answered.

Chapter Eleven

MIDNIGHT AND MY ALARM BEEPED on the nightstand. My pack was right next to my bed and I'd slept in my clothes. In one solid motion I shut off the alarm, got out of the bed and slung my pack over my shoulder. About two seconds later I knocked loudly on Black's door.

He answered the door. "You're kidding, right?"

"Nope. It's tomorrow. See you in about sixteen hours."

He checked his watch. "At least we'll still have some light when we start. Remember, don't leave the grid and no more than five dead within the first hour."

"Don't worry. I know the rules. See ya." I strutted away.

Though confident on the outside, I knew they'd probably find me shortly after my first shot. It was just a matter of how many I could take in one sitting.

As I hiked from the compound, my mind wandered for the first time since we'd started this training. I wondered what White was up to. I'd only been gone two weeks, but I missed him. Then my mind flitted to a vision of my laptop in my closet. I'd have to buy a new laptop when I got home. I knew I couldn't open my old one again without delving back into my earlier project and I didn't want to disappoint White by breaking a promise.

He remained on my mind throughout the night. I thought a lot about our next encounter and those thoughts kept me moving at a steady pace. The moon was waning and I'd be stuck out here in the dark in a couple of days. But, even though the light from the moon was almost non-existent, I made good progress. Black and I had been all over the map for the past two weeks and I knew the area better than I knew the terrain around the company cabin I'd spent so much time at.

My plan was simple. I wouldn't worry about the traces I left behind because I didn't plan on staying in my first location for more than a few seconds after I took my first shot. I'd try to cover my tracks so it would slow them as they tracked me. I refined my plan as I hiked and became more confident. The long arm of the sniper rifle could be my savior, as long as I was able to keep moving and found a good line of sight.

Real .50 caliber bullets would rip through trees and maybe even rock to reach my targets. The laser on this rifle might be hindered by something as flimsy as a leaf. Yet, I didn't have to consider ballistics. As long as I had a line of sight, I could take my target. I kept chanting in my mind, "Aim big, no head shots." I'd had to readjust my sites with almost every shot I'd taken over the past two weeks. "One shot, one kill," was still my mantra, but the prey was different. The best kill shot was the trunk of the body instead of the head. My intended victims wore no sensors on their heads. Though this had been fun, I'd have to let my partners know that this kind of training probably shouldn't be utilized too often or the men might get used to the simplicity of shooting the laser rifles.

The sun started to rise and I slowed my pace so I could pay more attention to where I put my feet. I didn't want to step on any wet earth, if I could help it. There was something mystical about moving through the forest and leaving no trace behind. My light steps made me feel as if I floated over the ground and my movements felt effortless as I took in the sunrise and the surrounding beauty of the mountains. I knew I was doing it right when I walked up on a doe and her fawn.

I drank in the scenery as I carefully made my way through the trees. Something about being out here alone felt so pure. Add in the impending game and the feeling became almost euphoric. This probably was as close to Heaven I'd get, so I might as well enjoy it while I was here. I'd questioned my role as Penumbra for various reasons but one of the biggest worries was how I'd explain myself to the powers that be, given the chance. I came to a realization as I glided through the forest. Black was right. I was made for this, so how could the powers that be deny me my reason for living?

I reached my first objective long before I expected Black to be marching into range. If he did it right, he'd set up camps that provided cover for his troops. He wouldn't let them mill about and he'd definitely have his own snipers on the lookout.

I'd not had any good sleep for days, but I seemed to have an endless supply of adrenaline. Though it seemed like a bottomless well, I knew it wasn't. I couldn't go on like this much longer so I forced myself to relax and nap against a tree.

When I woke early that evening, I took in my surroundings. The nice thing about the area we were working in was that the outward edge of the grid was rimmed with mountains in a horseshoe with smaller hills and plenty of clearings inside. I'd made the middle of the outer rim earlier and could see the entire basin. We'd narrowed the playing field some from the larger area we'd been playing on these past weeks and I almost wished I hadn't agreed on that. The more room the better off I'd be. But, I'd have to live with the agreement now.

My search rewarded me with a clear view of Black's army making a base camp not far from the first weapons cache tower of our prior missions. Obviously, Black had taken the outer ridge into consideration and had his troops set up their tents in a wall that blocked my line of sight quite well, but I still saw men on the edges of camp moving around. I worried about my lack of camouflage and hoped my position behind thick shrubs would be sufficient to conceal me.

After five minutes of studying his camp I searched for his snipers and found two right away. They didn't have the benefit of high ground yet and, were far enough away from camp that the men might still have a sense of security behind the tents before I started in on them. I worked quickly and took out the sniper the farthest from camp. *Forty left.* I made a mental note.

I refocused on camp Black and watched everyone scramble around a bit before I clicked off another shot. *Thirty-nine.*

I was well outside the first hour restrictions of only taking out five men, but I figured since this was for fun I'd count off five and wait an hour before trying for anymore. Three guys near the edges of camp heard their alarms in short order and I lost sight of the men after that. *Thirty-six.*

I used the next hour to relocate to a better vantage point. I had to get eyes on camp and do a head count. If Black was serious, I'd have some determined trackers on my trail while the bulk of the men drew my fire at camp. I had the benefit of a sixteen-hour head start, but they had the benefit of starting their hunt in daylight. It wouldn't take them long to cover what I'd done in the dark. I could only hope I'd get out of here in time.

I made good progress in that hour, considering I still tried to keep my location secret. I stopped to get my bearings and check for any easy targets. The camp was in my binoculars and I could see a lot more detail from here. Yet, I didn't get more than cursory glimpses of a few men. The sniper was gone from his previous location and I was getting nervous.

My search of the entire basin revealed a few men slinking through the brush, trying to locate my trail. I picked them off as soon as I located them. *Thirty.*

Only those six trackers, but where was Black? I didn't expect he'd be back at camp. He was a hands-on kind of guy. I worked my way around the ridge throughout the night. I needed full eyes on that camp.

With the light almost non-existent, my movements were extra careful and I moved slowly. I took out my night-vision goggles and picked up my pace a little more.

Just as the sun lit the sky I was on the backside of the camp. The elevation was fairly level in this part of the basin but the trees were dense. This forced me to move in closer. I considered finding a hiding spot until dark, but the thought of a wasted day and infrared made me take the chance of getting closer to camp so I could see what was going on.

I got within one hundred yards of camp Black and I could clearly hear them talking while I did my head count. Only four men. They had a table set up in one of the open fronted tents and played cards. Every couple of minutes one or two of them would get up and walk around, trying to look busy. It was quite the show.

My pistol slid quietly out of the holster as I stepped gently closer to camp. The four continued to play cards while I made my slow advance. I snuck as close as I dared. They continued to simulate activity every two minutes. I waited until all four of them were comfortable at the table again and then squeezed off four rounds. *Twenty-six.*

Alarms blared. One of the men had drawn his pistol, but the others knew they were out of the game and struggled to shut off the piercing sirens. I waited a few seconds to make sure no other men would come out of the tents. I had no idea if Black had men watching camp from a distance. If I ventured in, I had to be quick.

I kept my pistol drawn and moved it from side to side as I cautiously entered the half circle of tents. The men I'd shot stood at attention when I came into view, but I ignored them, they were dead. One of the rules I'd insisted on, once dead, the men could not talk or give any clues that might help the others figure out anything about me or my location.

Each man had a radio strapped to his belt. That was something I wanted. I yanked the radio from the first man I came to and switched it on. I immediately did a quick check of the remaining tents, throwing back flaps on the ones that were closed.

One of the tents housed several boxes stacked two high. I assumed they were supplies. Rummaging through the boxes yielded nothing worth carting around.

I was exiting the tent when Black's voice came through the radio. "Teams report."

The men I'd just shot were all watching me, but not moving from their current locations.

"Team One Recon," came over the radio. Then, "Team One Base reporting in." It went down the line just like that, skipping Team Three Recon and Team Three Base and ended with Team Five Base.

"All eyes on camp." Black's voice ordered. Damn, I had to get out of there.

I hurried out of camp. I stowed my pistol back into its holster, turned the volume down to barely audible on the radio and readied my rifle again. I'd hoped they'd talk a little more. Maybe give up a location or two, but I had no such luck.

Black still had twenty-six men at his disposal and they were all hunting me. The only option now was to start tracking them, one at a time.

I started by looking for traces leading from camp. It was tough going because I had to stay under cover. The men had enough time to get situated on the ridge I'd been shooting from yesterday and I knew they'd have a good line of sight if I ventured too far out. However, that's exactly where the trails led.

If base camp was just a decoy, Black had probably distributed the men out in a search grid and they probably pushed toward the ridge, trying to flush me out.

My attack on camp might have alerted them to my location behind them. However, having a radio was a definite advantage. They obviously didn't know that piece of info yet because they hadn't called radio silence.

Our men were good but I found enough evidence to make me believe I headed in the right direction. My progress was tedious but about two hours later I happened upon a group of four. They searched for traces of me and carried automatic rifles at the ready.

I hadn't been on this side of the grid yet, so I knew anything they found wouldn't be mine. I watched them for a couple of minutes and prepared to take them when Black's voice came over the radio.

"Report."

I guessed he called for a report every two hours.

The men in front of me stopped and one of them held his radio to his mouth. "Team One Recon, reporting no signs."

There was a short pause then I heard, "Team One Base reporting. No signs yet." Then identical reports came in for Team Two Recon, Team Two Base, Team Four Recon, Team Four Base, Team Five Recon, and Team Five Base. Again, I didn't hear anything from Team Three at all. They must have been either the six men I took out as they made their way across the grid or the men at camp. I assumed this meant that Black still had four teams of six. The teams were split in two. One group of four scouts, the recon team, and I assumed the base teams were a sniper and spotter in place to watch their backs. That meant I could easily be in a snipers line of sight.

The map of the area came to mind and I worked through it. With what I knew already, I thought I had Black's plan figured out.

I was on the northeastern edge of the grid and decided to leave these four men intact until I could locate their sniper and spotter. I wasn't far from the location I thought would be best for them to set up. I worked my way to the very edge of the grid and worked along the outer edge as quickly and quietly as possible. Thankfully, I found the two men right where I thought they'd be. I skirted their position until I was directly behind them. Getting as close as I dared, I pulled out my pistol and took them out.

"Don't move. You're dead," I said over the alarms as I hurried into their little hide.

The worst part about this was that the men, though out of commission, didn't stop moving like a real dead person would. I dove between them and pulled the sniper rifle away from one of the men. His was already pointing in the direction I wanted to look. I wasn't disappointed and located the four men I'd walked away from a few minutes ago. They obviously didn't hear their teammate's alarms because they still scoured their surroundings.

My decision was made. It would only be two hours before the next radio check, so that meant I had to hurry. I took them all out in short order. *Twenty* .

I searched the opposite ridgeline and was rewarded with another sniper and spotter. I took them down and then searched below them in an imagined grid. Four more men were easily spotted as they searched. They were out of the game before I took my next breath. *Fourteen.*

I didn't hang out with the dead men but looked back as I walked away and gave them a nod and a grin.

I was as certain as I could be, without being in on the plan, that I knew where each team was located. Time would be my enemy now. I had to get to the next team before they reported in and I only had about an hour and a half if my guess was right. It was going to be close. Then, I'd have to change my tactics because they'd know my heading. If I could move fast, I could take out everyone with exception of Black and the extra sniper I'd missed back near camp.

By the time I reached the next sniper and spotter I'd shut off my radio. I certainly didn't want to alert them to my presence when the call for reports came out. I knew I only had a matter of minutes. I took them out with my pistol, exactly as I'd taken out the previous team and repeated the rest of the motions of locating their scouting team, removing them from the picture and locating the two on the opposite ridge and their scouting team. It was done within seconds of the next call for reports. *Two left.*

The radio came on, "Report." There was a full ten seconds of silence before Black called for the report once again with the same result.

One of the men I'd just taken out let out a low whistle making me remember he really wasn't dead. The other one responded to the whistle with, "Holy shit. Are you serious?"

"Empty your pockets and packs, boys." I demanded.

This was something I should have done at camp. But, Black calling for a report put me in a hurry. Actually, it worked out for the best because I made it to the two other team bases just in time to get everyone before they knew what was going on. Now, there was no way to ferret out where I was by analyzing my shot order.

I found the map that should have been given to each team leader with the grid and realized that what I'd called camp Black was Team Six, so Team Three must have been the men I took out at first. The extra sniper must be with Black. If they didn't split up, I'd have a better chance. I wished I'd had this map earlier and I would have known I was right about the plan before I gambled. Thankfully, it had worked out.

Unfortunately, Black didn't have a grid for himself and neither was his role spelled out for me. The only thing I could think to do was return back to camp Black and start running down the trails that led away from there.

It was dark before I got back to camp, so I hung back and took a short nap. The men talked and their relaxed chatting lulled me to sleep. When they turned quiet, I woke up. I scanned camp for a living member of the army but the men had stopped talking because they'd gone to sleep and not because someone was investigating and they couldn't talk.

I still had a couple hours before the sun rose and I couldn't do any good tracking in the dark, so I took this time to dig into an MRE. They always tasted better after a couple days out in the field.

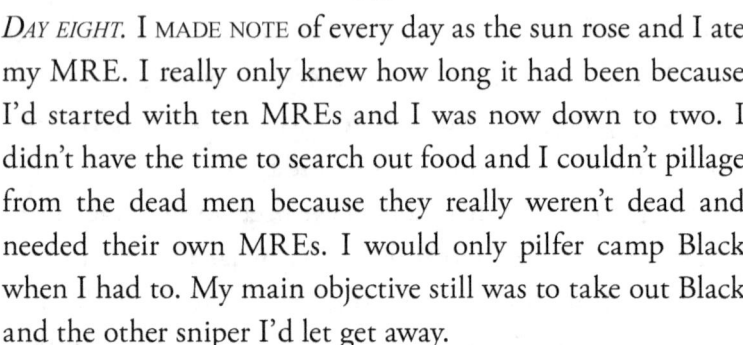

DAY EIGHT. I MADE NOTE of every day as the sun rose and I ate my MRE. I really only knew how long it had been because I'd started with ten MREs and I was now down to two. I didn't have the time to search out food and I couldn't pillage from the dead men because they really weren't dead and needed their own MREs. I would only pilfer camp Black when I had to. My main objective still was to take out Black and the other sniper I'd let get away.

I'd spent the last six days running down all the different trails leading through the grid. The men were getting fidgety because they were required to stay dead at their exact locations. Of course, they'd get up and roam around their immediate area and this made my tracking efforts harder. But, passing the nights had been brutal. In my mind, every sound was Black sneaking up on me. The silence was even worse because I had nowhere to focus my attentions. I spent a good part of my day finding a place to sleep, but I didn't sleep well. At least I knew every crevice and hole that I could fit into by now.

Every time I'd come upon a death scene the men would scramble back to their place of death and stand at attention. I found it funny and started looking forward to walking in among the dead. That was until I got near the death scene for the sniper and spotter in sector two. Thankfully, I'd come across the spotter just as he zipped up after relieving himself. I made him walk in front of me back toward the hide. As expected, the sniper stood at attention when he saw us coming. When we drew nearer, the alarm in a pack near the sniper sounded and I bolted back toward cover.

As soon as I got under cover, I double-checked my alarm, but it was silent. I'd gotten lucky. I didn't know if Black or the other sniper had missed their mark and shot the man in front of me, but I decided to avoid the dead from then on out.

For the shooter to have missed his target, me, he had to have been shooting from a position that didn't afford him the best line of site as I walked toward the sniper hide. It's possible I would be dead if that had been a real bullet. I worked through the map in my mind again. I didn't dare move much and draw attention to my hiding spot. The area was fairly large, but at least now I knew about where one of the remaining shooters was located.

I was still working through how I was going to get out of there when I heard an unfamiliar voice over the radio, "Sector Two, Commander."

"Confirmed kill?" Black's voice came to me next.

"No sir. But, she's still there."

I knew Black would be watching now or on his way toward me. I had to be extra careful. I started a low crawl out of there. It was a risk I absolutely had to take. They had my location, but I had the other snipers location narrowed down. I hoped he'd stay put.

I wasn't far from base camp, which wasn't far from the tower. The tower marked their rendezvous point and probably where the shooter hid and had been hiding since day one. I wish I'd have thought of this before. Instead, I ignored the tower because it was someplace that would be hard to defend from snipers on the higher ridges.

I'd made my way slowly to the top of the ridge and decided to make a run for it. This was part of the map where the backside of the ridge was still in play. I had to get behind the ridge or Black would find me crawling around on the forest floor.

"Movement at the top of the ridge," I heard the man say. "She's behind the ridge, moving west. I have no shot."

"Keep me up to date," Black said.

His voice was strained and came in a single breath. It sounded as though he was running.

Damn it! He knew exactly where I was and in what direction I was headed. I doubled back and followed the backside of the ridge toward my very first hide. I didn't care about my tracks at the moment. I had to put some distance between my last known location and me.

Because I ran flat out, I made my destination in less than an hour. I fell to the ground and crested the ridge on my belly. My view wouldn't be the best until I got onto the downward slope. My muscles screamed to take it slow but my brain pushed me to crawl as fast as I could.

My rifle was ready before I had eyes on the tower, so when I could finally see it, I was ready to do my scan. I wasn't disappointed and saw my target sweeping with his binoculars. Not a smart move. As with all my shots, time stood still and I watched him locate me in the binoculars.

He dropped the binoculars, tried to ready his own rifle and use the radio at the same time. He did manage, "Sector..." before his alarm blared through the radio. Of course, he was already in the process of speaking and the word Three came out as well. Again, Black knew my location. At least this time he didn't know exactly where I was in the grid.

I jumped up and moved down the ridge to a crevice I'd slept in three nights ago. It jutted back into the hillside a couple feet but was too tight for me to utilize my rifle. Less than five minutes after I got settled I heard rustling above. My heart leapt into my throat. A good tracker like Black would have no trouble figuring out where I hid.

My pistol was at the ready as I waited for Black to show himself. It seemed like hours before he pounced. Our alarms went off at the same time.

"Damn."

Black pulled his pack from his back and switched off his alarm. My alarm was still blaring and in the tight space it was almost more than I could stand. I struggled to work myself out of the hole and Black leaned down and offered me a hand. I was dragged out of the hole in one short pull. I followed Black's lead and shut off my alarm.

As soon as it was quiet, Black stuck out his hand. I took it and he gave me that gruff shake I'd seen him do with all the other men. He literally lifted me from the ground as he pulled me in for a quick embrace.

"Nice," was all that he said as he set me back down. Then he spoke into the radio, "Game over, men. Rendezvous at camp in sector six. As soon as we break camp we'll return home."

"So? Who got who first?" I asked.

"Doesn't matter. They were both kill shots and fired almost simultaneously. We both would have had time to pull the trigger."

We were back at camp Black within two hours and the men already had everything ready to be hauled back out of the forest. Again, we were saluted as soon as we walked into camp. One of the men asked, "Who won?"

"Forty-one, Grey. One, Team Black." Black answered the question.

The looks made me very self-conscious but I held my head high.

The man I'd taken out in the tower walked toward me with a somber expression. When he was directly in front of me he held out his hand. I took it.

"Great game, Commander."

"It was fun," I replied.

Black and I grabbed some of the supplies and led the way back to the compound. The hike back was light and easy, even though we pushed hard. Most of the army had been just sitting out here for eight days with nothing much to do but play dead. Their speed mixed with the carefree attitude convinced me they were ready to return to the compound.

Chapter Twelve

WE MADE IT BACK TO the compound late that afternoon.

"We get real food tonight." Black pointed toward the mess hall as we marched back onto the compound. He addressed the men, thanking them for participating. I expected him to berate them for not winning and asked him about it after we left them.

"It was more the fault of the planner," his voice was disappointed. "I shouldn't have kept them in such large groups. The next time around, I'll do better."

"What do you mean? Next time. I have no intentions of being hunted by forty men at one time again."

"You never know what might come up when you're out in the field." We stood outside my apartment door in Headquarters.

"Maybe. Just know I won't be doing it again any time soon. I'm exhausted." I left him standing in the hall.

THE FIRST THING I DID was shower. The hot water felt so good. I stood under the spray watching the mud circle the drain. It was a full five minutes before the water became clear again, making me lose interest. I hadn't been that dirty for months and something about it was satisfying. I'd finally gotten my hands dirty again.

The mess hall wasn't far from Headquarters. Black sat alone at the officer's table and indicated a full plate of food to his left. The tables filled the room in orderly rows. Black's army was spread out at the tables, intermingled with new faces. I watched as one of the men, who hadn't been involved in the recent training, picked up a biscuit and brought it to his mouth. The sniper from sector two smacked it from his hand and some harsh words were exchanged. The would be biscuit eater was going to get belligerent, but more men stood from their seats to back the sniper. That's when I noticed that none of them ate, even though they all had full plates in front of them.

"Did you get this for me?" I asked before I sat down.

"Yep."

I took a seat and looked around the room. All eyes were on us.

"What's going on?" I asked Black.

"They won't eat until you do. It's a show of respect."

I immediately picked up my own biscuit and took a bite. It was heavenly and I savored it as I watched everyone finally dig in. Conversations started to spring up here and there and it sounded like a regular mess hall before I finished my biscuit.

Black and I sat alone at the officer's table and neither of us said anything. I watched the conversations as I ate. I had tried to break myself of the habit of eavesdropping, but it had become automatic, like reading.

The conversations were all the same. It was all a retelling of our training op. The men kept looking at our table while they talked, so even if I couldn't read lips, I would have known they talked about us.

After dinner I went straight to bed and didn't wake up until late the next morning when Black knocked at my door, looking for coffee.

"Sleep well?" He asked as he sat down at my table.

"Too well." I rubbed my eyes and yawned as I started the coffee brewing.

"Brown will be here sometime this afternoon or evening and we'll leave for the office tomorrow."

The mention of going home brought White to the front of my thoughts. He was always there, but I'd been purposefully ignoring those thoughts while I worked. I looked forward to seeing him, but I was worried. I hadn't been away from him for any length of time for several months and now I'd been gone almost a full month. I'd asked for it and needed it, but was it what White and I needed? What had he been doing while I was gone? Did he even think of me now that he'd had a taste? I wanted to believe that his loyalty ran as deep for me as mine for him, but he was a man. All of my experiences with men made me worry that he'd lose interest if I were out of sight. I pushed the worry down and decided it might not be a bad idea to hang out in the office for a few days or even a couple weeks.

Black and I spent the rest of the day wandering around the compound, checking things out. We hadn't taken a proper tour of this compound yet and took advantage of our time before Brown arrived.

I tried to ignore the conversations not meant for our ears or my eyes. Still, I caught enough snippets to know our recent training op was still the main topic. I finally came to the conclusion I should have given in and let the men get me right away. It wasn't just the awe or disbelief that had me self-conscious. It felt as if my relationship with Black had changed as well. He walked around with extreme pride evident on his face but no longer had that teacher's air. I suppose being considered an equal to Black could be a good thing, but I'd always looked up to him as a type of mentor and liked that he seemed to keep me under his wing. Now, I was afraid he might stop backing me as much as he used to.

LATER THAT AFTERNOON BLACK AND I met Brown at the airstrip. Red had come along with him.

"Heard about your exploits, Ms. Grey." Red's voice held notes of condescension and superiority.

I just nodded and smiled. I didn't know where he was going with this, but I was certain I wouldn't like it. It was possible he could be making conversation. He did have a tendency to try to make everyone feel inferior when he spoke. Yet, the glint in his eye made me suspect him of prodding and I hated prodding.

"When did you take up sniper jobs on the side?" He questioned.

My mental warning light was already flashing but this intensified it. I just shook my head and laughed it off. Still, there was a definite air of accusation to his words. I hoped Red was just being a jerk and had no real idea who I was. I tried to make sure the tension I felt didn't spill over into my body language.

"Seriously? When?" He kept at it.

I gave in and faced him with raised eyebrows. I stood with my legs slightly spread and solid, as if I were about to take a punch. As soon as I took the stance I knew I'd screwed up. That's exactly what Red was looking for and the look of triumph on his face was too much.

"Screw off, Red."

I forced myself to relax. I hoped I could blow it off as him just pissing me off instead of me having something to hide. The uncomfortable looks from Black and Brown told me they both felt the stress of the situation.

"Don't start fights, Red," Black said.

At least now I knew he'd still come to my defense. I just wished it hadn't been when I was trying to hide something from him, too.

"She's been too busy playing White's nurse maid," Brown jabbed.

He, obviously, had no idea what exactly White and I had done on our last job. I gave him the expected disapproving look and he grinned. I felt sick. Red let it drop but I could picture the wheels turning in his head and I didn't like it one bit.

My feelings of guilt made me go directly to my room after dinner while the boys went to the compound bar for a couple of drinks. I'd lied to my partners without saying anything, twice. And, what made it worse was that two of the three had defended my lies.

I didn't sleep well that night and was already on my fourth cup of coffee when Black came to my door the next morning.

He took his seat at the table and waited for his coffee before he said, "We'll leave in about an hour. You packed?"

"I didn't bring any luggage, remember?" I only managed a slight smile.

"Everything okay?"

"Yeah. I didn't sleep well, that's all."

About half an hour later Red showed up at my door. "I thought I'd find him here." He nodded at Black.

You just have to make sure I know you're not *here to see me.*

I raised my eyebrows and scowled at him.

"May I join you for coffee?"

I opted to let him in because Red and I had made huge strides over the last year or so and I'd begun to think of him as just another one of the guys. But, now that his curiosity was obviously piqued, I didn't trust him, and he was being an overall jerk. I had no excuse other than general dislike to deny him entry, but that didn't mean I had to be overly cordial.

"Go ahead and get yourself a cup." I pointed to the brewed coffee. There was no way I was going to wait on him after his nasty attitude.

Brown showed up shortly after Red had gotten his own coffee. I immediately poured him a cup and delivered it with a smile. The gesture wasn't lost on any of the men. Red's smug amusement shown on his face and only served to irk me further.

"So," Red directed at me. "Are we going to start putting you out on hit jobs?"

"Do we even do that?" I raised my eyebrows at him in a challenge.

"At times, but with your skills we could take on more." He returned the challenging look from across the table.

"Nah. Not my style." I directed all of my attention into my coffee cup.

Black attempted to redirect the conversation by asking how things were going at the office.

"Nothing new." Red gave me a sidelong glance that I pretended I didn't see. "And, you." He pointed a finger at Black. "Even *you* couldn't track her? Man, you had eight days."

"What's your problem, Red?" Black asked, his jaw tightening.

"It all just seems a little contrived."

I'd heard enough.

"So you think we set it up? One little girl couldn't do what I did? There's no way I could take out forty men *and* Black? You're right Red. We set it up. Black thought the men should show more respect for their female co-workers. Funny, it didn't carry over to you. Honestly, I couldn't figure out how to pull the trigger on those damned fire sticks." I was on the verge of standing from my seat and smacking the smug look from his face.

"So what if she's good at something, man. What's the big deal?" Brown backed me. "We've all seen her shoot that sniper rifle. And," he continued, "Black taught her how to get around the woods. There's nothing unbelievable about this. Sounds like you're just trying to get your ass kicked."

Brown's hackles were raised. I'd only seen this side of him a handful of times. I loved that he'd take my side over Red's, but the guilt gnawed at me.

"Ha. *You're* going to kick my ass?" Red challenged Brown.

I was tense and waited for one of them to stand from his seat. That would be my cue. Brown and Black would *not* fight my fight. I didn't know if I could take Red or not, but I'd give it a shot.

"I don't think I'd be fast enough to either kick your ass or protect your ass if it comes to blows."

The intensity in Brown's eyes gave a different meaning to his smile.

Red faced me, as if waiting for his very own black eye. I ran through all the fight scenarios and seriously considered acting them out. I really wanted to break his nose, but I knew it was wrong. He was my partner, even if I didn't care for him. This wouldn't be anything like me popping Brown to make a point. There was an actual grudge I'd be fighting and that was entirely different.

"I think we've exhausted this subject. I'll meet you all at the airfield in fifteen."

Red slowly stood from his chair, indicating he didn't want to get physical. Though his tone was sincere his eyes still held suspicion. I expected him to add something else to his last statement, but it never came. Instead, he left the three of us sitting uncomfortably in my room.

I figured this wouldn't be the end of it, but at least it was the end of this round.

As we boarded the chopper I noticed Red had left the tension in his shoulders behind.

The flight was only slightly awkward for me. I tried to figure out what had prompted Red to get so riled up about my good showing on the field. My mind went directly to Penumbra. I had to protect her at all costs, even from my partners. But, that was my problem. If I weren't Penumbra, I knew that would be the last thing on my mind. I had to forget about her when talking to Red. Penumbra did not exist in my world, at least not intimately. Still, what did he think he knew? I hadn't done a Penumbra job since Dimitri and Red had no clue back then. He couldn't know, I reassured myself and dozed in my seat.

NONE OF US HAD BAGS to deposit in our rooms so we all went directly to the office to check in with White.

Gabriella greeted us all with a smile and a nod as we walked past her into White's office.

"How'd things go?" White asked when we each took a seat.

"Great," Black answered.

"Glad to have you home, Ms. Grey, but I don't need you at the moment," White said as soon as I'd gotten comfortable.

I didn't know how to take this. Was I still being talked about behind closed doors or were they going to discuss something else? I left gracefully, though I wanted to stomp to the door and slam it when I left.

"That was quick," Gabriella said.

"I was kicked out." I slumped in my chair.

"What? Why?"

"No idea." I shrugged.

"Wonder what's going on?" she asked.

"I suppose, they're either on some secret mission or I'm the topic at hand."

"Speaking of—" Gabriella grew a large smile. "Did you really get the best of *Black* ?"

"No. We killed each other. It was a draw." I grinned at the thought. "It was really fun."

I got lost in my own descriptions as I spent the next twenty minutes telling her all about how Black and I took out teams of ten as partners and then how Black wanted to test my skills by pitting me against all of the men at once.

"I've definitely got the better job," she said when I took a breath.

"No you don't." I argued.

"Yes I do, sweetie. I got to eat real food more than a few times in the past month. Marty took me to the movies twice. I slept in a real bed. Not to mention, I showered regular."

"Haven't you ever been camping?"

"Yes, I have. I'd rather be in the city." She waved away the idea of camping with a flick of her wrist.

"The beauty of the mountains—"

"No, honey. Not going to convince me. Not even with that dreamy look you're wearing. I prefer to see the mountains in scenery pictures or from the car as we drive to the hotel."

We laughed.

"Why do we get along so well?" I asked.

"Because I'm perfect and you're awesome," she said without having to even think about it.

I stood. "So true. I'll be in my apartment if anyone wants me." I hiked my head toward White's office and rolled my eyes.

"I'll let him know."

I ORDERED IN CHINESE FOOD for dinner and ordered extra just in case someone came knocking at my door. I ended up eating alone and more than I should have and fell asleep on the couch.

Black showed up the next morning for coffee.

"I won't be going to the gym for a while," he said.

"Where're you going?"

"No where. I'll still be here to drink your coffee."

He stayed for several quiet cups before he left me alone. We rarely experienced uncomfortable silence. Was that why he came to me for his morning coffee? I had to admit, having another person to share my morning coffee with was nice and not having to make conversation first thing in the morning just added to my satisfaction level.

By late morning I wondered why White hadn't called or shown up at my door yet. I had been gone a month and he had no desire to catch up? Even if we hadn't taken that leap into a more involved relationship, I would have been offended. I didn't want to come off as a needy girlfriend so I hesitated to pick up the phone. How was I supposed to act? Were we really calling each other boyfriend and girlfriend? What did that mean, anyway? The titles seemed so juvenile, somehow. But, what else was there? Lovers? I couldn't really bring myself to use that terminology. Once didn't really count for anything other than a good time. I hated this. I paced for half an hour before I picked up my phone. There was no point in putting it off and worrying for days. I'd given him my soul and I deserved to know what was going on between us.

Gabriella transferred me directly to White.

"Yes?"

"Hey. What are you doing?" I wanted to slap myself for not coming up with something better.

"Working." I heard papers being shuffled around.

"I thought you might have stopped in yesterday or found some time in your schedule to welcome me home."

"I'm sorry, babe. I've just been really busy. I've got something lined up for you, though. I figure, if we're both busy, the time apart will pass easier."

I grinned from ear to ear. He called me babe. Maybe he wasn't blowing me off.

"We haven't had any time alone since *Carmen's Retreat* ." I didn't want him to think I was being possessive or overbearing, even if I felt like I was. However, a month is a long time to be apart. It wasn't out of line expecting a, ' *I missed you.'*

"I know and it's going to be a while yet. Can you come down in a bit?"

"Sure. I'll be down in about an hour." I hung up and took a deep breath. I was ready in less than half an hour and found myself outside the main office door before I thought about how it might look.

I stepped in anyway and took some time to chat with Gabriella.

"What brings you here in such a good mood?"

"White asked me to come down. Maybe he has a job for me. I really hate sitting around."

"I'm sure it's not just a possible job that's got you all excited," she smirked.

"What?" I feigned innocence. "I guess maybe I'm a little excited to see him. It's been a month."

"You can't let him see you this excited." She gave me a level look.

I took some deep breaths to calm myself but was only able to contain the smile slightly.

"Are you ready?" Her finger hovered over the intercom button.

"No. I have half an hour yet before I'm supposed to meet him."

She laughed. "Half an hour early, too. I hope he appreciates what he's got."

Though I hadn't told Gabriella about our encounter on the yacht, she could always read me when it came to my feelings about White.

The half an hour at Gabriella's desk seemed to take days. Finally, it was time to announce me.

"Ms. Grey is here."

"Send her right in." He sounded happy through the phone intercom.

After a couple more deep breaths I entered his office.

"Hey." He smiled and gestured to a chair in front of his desk.

We visited for several minutes before he finally brought up the training op in Wyoming.

"Your prowess as a sniper has Red's panties in a bunch."

"I know. I probably shouldn't have tried as hard as I did."

"Probably. But we can't change it now. What I've got is a Penumbra contract."

He pushed an envelope across the desk toward me.

The target was Lucio Flores of Peru. His daily routine and upcoming appointments were all provided as well as a map of Peru's capital city of Lima. His job title wasn't listed, but the appointments suggested he was some sort of government official.

"This is an urban hit." I passed the map to White.

"Looks like it. You feel up to it?"

"I've never done anything in an urban setting." I bordered on panic with this prospect.

"If you're uncomfortable with this, we can decline."

"Where does this request come from?"

"I don't know, for sure. I ran it past your father, just in case, and he's given his blessing. Does that help?"

"A little. I better do some research before I decide. There's no reason listed and I have no idea who this guy is."

"He's head of border security and has been letting drugs cross the borders. At least that's what the Admiral tells me."

"Sounds like even if dad isn't paying for this job, he's involved."

"That's my impression." White shrugged.

"I still want to do a little research, to be sure," I said.

"Of course. Let me know as soon as you can. This is time sensitive." He stood and came around the desk while he dug in his pocket. He pulled out his keys and held them out for me. "You can use C.I.C."

"Thanks."

I reached out for his keys and our hands touched. My breath caught in my throat as his hand enveloped mine. The keys felt sharp in my hand as he held me there. I didn't complain about the pain, it was the only thing keeping me from losing all sense of location.

"Can we do dinner tonight?" His voice was eager.

I tried to swallow, but my mouth had gone dry. Instead, I gulped in some air. White's expression had become predatory but I managed a slight nod.

"I'll meet you in my apartment at six o'clock, then?"

"Okay." I managed to keep my voice clear and steady and lifted my chin as I walked out of the office.

I met Red in the front office as I was leaving. I still wasn't fully composed but Red's presence helped me refocus my thoughts immensely.

"What's that?" He indicated the envelope. His bearing was that of an officer challenging one of his recruits.

I scrutinized it while turning it over in my hands then said, "Huh? It's an envelope."

Red's expression changed from superior to annoyed. I smiled pleasantly at him and Gabriella as I walked out of the office. As soon as I had the office door shut behind me my smile turned from pleasant to beaming and I carried it all the way up to White's apartment. It didn't drop away until I put the key into the lock. Then, my hands started to tremble as I remembered White's demeanor toward me less than two minutes earlier. I had to take several deep breaths to calm myself enough to get the door open.

Once inside the apartment I went directly to C.I.C. and fell into a chair in front of a computer. My imagination took over and I had to force myself to focus long enough to turn on the machine in front of me. White had always had a strong effect on me, but now his hold was even stronger. I was looking forward to six o'clock and had to fight with myself to concentrate.

Researching Lucio Flores had taken less than an hour before I had enough information to convince me that the job was in the interest of all things good. I also found out Flores was connected to Mateo Ruiz and his efforts to reestablish a formidable drug cartel. This could be a way to get involved in what the guys wouldn't talk about in front of me.

White's attention had dwindled, and his workload had skyrocketed since our encounter in Jamaica. Though I had no proof, I knew my partners were working on a job that involved Mateo Ruiz and the mysterious man we saw eating lunch with Ruiz.

All I really knew was that White and I had inadvertently stumbled upon some bad guy the government wanted to get their hands on, and that guy also had connections to Mateo Ruiz. The more involved I got with Ruiz, the better. At least I wasn't breaking my promise not to pry if I got my information this way. My current research was legitimate and maybe it could help me figure out what else was going on.

I sat back in my chair, pleased with my progress and checked my watch. It was nowhere near six o'clock. I changed my task to that of planning. I had never done much of anything in an urban setting and questioned my ability. This scared me.

The Dimitri hit could be considered urban, I reminded myself. This helped to settle my unease, and I was able to concentrate and start making some definite plans.

I had several options open to me, but one of the big questions was whether or not to do the hit in a public area or try and take him in a more private setting. I also had to worry about acquiring a weapon locally. Penumbra's signature weapon might be a .50 cal. sniper rifle, but it was not the only way she was known to complete her objective.

I got up from the computer and called White.

"Yes?" His voice came through to my ear.

"Does Helix have connections in Peru?" I asked.

"I'm sure he does—"

"Do you think you can get him to set up a way for me to my hardware?"

"Yep. Where do you want to pick it up?" He was short and to the point.

"Lima. I'd do it myself, but you took his phone number from me."

He chuckled. "I did, didn't I? Okay. I'm still with Red. I'll call you back in a while."

We hung up and I went back to making plans. I wanted to get this done and get back as soon as I could, so I made my travel reservations. My flight left late tomorrow morning. I only hoped White would be able to talk Helix into setting up a weapon for me.

Lucio's schedule was fairly routine and slightly rigid. That always helped. If a person had habits, I could use them against them instead of wondering where they might be at any given time of day. The best plan, on paper, was taking him at home. I spent a good amount of time locating his apartment building via satellite and finding a nearby building I could easily gain access to. I systematically planned his death according to his own schedule. I was into the second week of his itinerary when I heard White's front door open. My heart skipped a beat and I found myself straightening my shirt and hair.

To avoid looking too eager, I remained in my seat with every intention of finishing up the specific scenario I was working on. About ten seconds later I finally gave in and turned around to look out the door of C.I.C.. Red stood in the doorway watching me.

"Grey. White asked me to tell you he'd be right up."

I casually turned away from him and shut off the computer. I didn't know how much he'd seen, but I'd had a big picture of Lima on the screen. The last thing I needed was for him to know where I'd be in the coming days.

"Thanks."

I rose from the computer and pushed past him. Coffee sounded good all of a sudden. When I turned from the coffee pot Red sat at White's kitchen bar with his hands folded in front of him. His head was cocked to one side and his expression was scrutinizing.

"What are you working on?" He asked.

"Just playing around and passing the time." I shrugged.

Red nodded, but wore a suspicious look. "Do you know what White has you up for next?"

"No. I don't think he has anything lined up. How about you? What are you doing?"

"Actually, I think he's going to send you off for EOD and flight training next. That should keep you busy for a few months."

He employed some of my father's tactics and ignored my question completely.

"Sounds good. When?" I let him get away with it to avoid an argument.

"Probably next week sometime. Brown's not happy with it, but that's the way it goes."

"Why isn't Brown happy with it?"

"He'll be instructing you and isn't quite ready to give up several months right now. He'll get over it." He smiled. "We haven't had much time to talk since White was shot. We've both been pretty busy. So, how have things been?"

"Good." I used the unintentional teachings of Black for shortest answer.

"Are you still happy in this job?" I knew he was trying his head shrinking techniques on me again.

"Now that I'm getting back to it, yes." Just a simple yes would have done, I berated myself.

"How was *Carmen's Retreat* ?"

"Beautiful. Did you know it has a garage with all kinds of watercraft? They roll them out of a door on the side of the yacht with hydraulics and lower them onto the water. It was really cool."

He smiled. I was onto his game and he knew it. "It's not a garage. It's called a bay. I heard you and White shared a suite. How did that go?"

My temperature raised but I kept it in check. "It sucked. It was a pain to have to change my clothes in the bathroom. It wasn't as roomy as a regular bathroom."

"You know what I like about you, Alex?"

"What's that?"

"You're a challenge. But I'll get there. I'd like to get back to where we were a couple months ago. You weren't so guarded. Why did you get so defensive back in Wyoming when I questioned you about your sniping and evasion tactics? Do you have something to hide?"

"Nothing to hide here. Why'd you revert back to prick-psychiatrist mode? You know I don't respond well to that."

"I guess I'm just a little suspicious of the time you and White have been spending together. Then he comes back from *Carmen's Retreat* and, though we have a pressing issue, he's more relaxed than I've seen him in more than a year."

"So you're taking White's issues out on me? Do you do that because I'm a woman and you think I'm easier to crack than he is? Or is it because he's your friend and I'm just an intrusion? Maybe it's because you have issues of your own? Whatever your problem is keep it to yourself from now on. If you want to *get back to where we were a couple months ago* don't come at me as if I'm the one with issues. I'm quite content."

"I don't know why I always forget to take the direct route with you." He folded his hands in front of himself. "Are you and White—" he looked toward the ceiling in thought for a few seconds, "a couple?" He chose the least offensive way to put it, which probably saved him a lot of grief.

I smiled. "There it is. Finally, you get to the point." I turned around and poured us each a cup of coffee. "You've told me in the past that the men's relationships are your business because— Actually, you never did convince me why it's any of your business, so there you go. It's none of your business whether or not I'm getting any and from where I choose to get it from." I said when I set his cup in front of him.

The door opened and White came in with our food.

"I got Italian. I hope that's okay." He set it down on the counter, not at all rattled Red was here. White maneuvered around me and grabbed plates and utensils for the three of us.

Despite my answer, Red watched us both closely as we ate. I thought we handled ourselves well during the meal. Afterward, I hoped Red would leave, but caught myself saying goodnight before he did. I felt antsy, and didn't want Red to pick up on it. If White really wanted to see me, he'd call when Red left.

The clock ticked off the hours as I sat on my couch, waiting for that call. By three A.M. I was tired of infomercials and was about to give up when the call finally came.

"Hello?"

"Red just left. He's been on my back all day."

"That's okay. We have to give up some things if we want to keep this a secret, I guess." I switched the topic. "Did you ever get in touch with Helix?"

"Not yet. I'll do that first thing in the morning."

"Good. My flight leaves around ten in the morning."

"You set it all up already?"

"Yep. I thought it'd be good to get it over and done with."

"You have a place to stay?"

"Of course."

"What about a return flight? When is it?"

"It's an open ticket, so I should be able to return any time for the next month."

"Good." He went down the list of preparations with me and discovered the only thing I hadn't covered was the weapon. "You've got it all under control, I guess."

"I'm ready to get back out there and yet, I'm ready to get back here as soon as possible."

"You might not be too happy with me, then." He sighed.

"Why?"

"I'm going to send you off for EOD and flight training when you get back."

"Red already told me. He said *several* months."

"EOD is a four month course." White said.

"Four months?" For some reason, the full implication of *several* hadn't connected in my brain to mean more than two.

"I know. It's something you should do and it'd be best to get it done. Besides, this will help alleviate some of Red's suspicions about us."

"He came right out and asked me if we were a couple." I said.

"What did you say?" White's question came quick.

"I told him it wasn't any of his business who I was sleeping with and then you walked in. That was good timing, by the way."

"I suppose." He sounded a little disappointed before he switched the conversation back to my training. "Brown will be taking over the EOD while you're there and I'm setting it up so Will can be your flight instructor."

"Will?" My stomach churned. I'd found myself extremely attracted to White's little brother and I didn't know how to handle this.

"Is that a problem?" White asked.

"No. It might be nice to get to know your brother a little better."

"He's a good instructor and I know you'll be trained right if he does it."

I nodded and remembered he couldn't see me through the phone. "Okay," I said.

"It doesn't look like we're going to get any time together before you leave. I'm sorry." He let out a long breath.

"It can't be helped."

"I'll call Helix first thing in the morning. Maybe we can get all of it set up before you take off, so be sure to check in with me before you leave if I haven't called you already."

"Sounds good."

We continued to talk and, before I was ready to hang up, Black knocked at my door for his morning coffee.

"You might have to do something about Black in the mornings," I said before I answered the door.

"Why?"

"He's here for his morning coffee and if I'm not here for a while, he'll know about it, unless you keep him busy in the mornings."

"Noted. I'll see what I can do."

I'd poured a cup of coffee and carried it to the door with me. "I better let him in. I'll talk to you later."

Black and I enjoyed a couple cups in silence. As soon as he left I packed and gave White a call right after I called for a cab to take me to the airport.

"Did you get in touch with Helix?" I asked after we'd done the customary greetings.

"It's all set." He gave me all the details. I was to go to a small gun shop and firing range and ask for Maria.

"Thanks. Hopefully, I'll be home in a couple days. Keep Black away from my apartment or make sure I know what you told him before I see him when I get back."

"Be safe."

"I will. Talk soon."

Chapter Thirteen

THE FLIGHT WAS UNEVENTFUL BUT the humidity hit me hard in the face when I stepped out of the airport to pick up my car. It was early evening when I got checked in, so I decided to order room service. While I waited for my food I readied my duffle bag for a long day. I included several bottles of water, a camera, iPad, and all of my cash.

The next morning I found the gun shop and firing range without any trouble. The main part of the building was filled with hunting gear but all of the weapons were locked up behind the counter and a man stood behind thick glass with a metal mesh imbedded inside. Signs directed my attention toward the firing range behind some solid metal doors. I didn't look around long before I asked the clerk for Maria.

"One moment, please." He turned and went into a room behind him.

The store was in good shape and, other than the ominous glass that separated me from the clerk, it was quite inviting. I had expected a dive since they were dealing in black market weapons. So much for presumptions, I thought as a slender woman with long black hair stepped out of the room.

"Can I help you?" Her eyes narrowed at me.

"Helix sent me to pick up something for a client," I answered.

Maria made her way to a steel door at the end of the counter and opened it wide for me. I followed her to the room she had just come from. Maria locked the door behind us and led me to the far corner of the room. Here she slid aside a copy machine and opened a trap door.

We descended into darkness but it didn't last long. She reached up and yanked on a pull string and the room was filled with a dim yellow light from a single bulb.

"Feel free to browse." She stepped aside, allowing me a full view of the room. It wasn't all that large and neither was her selection.

I went directly to the rifles and inspected them.

"What are you looking for?" Maria's voice cut the silence.

"My client just wants a rifle."

I picked one of them up. It came with a scope and that was a plus.

"That's a .308. Made in Brazil."

"How do they handle?" I brought it to my shoulder.

"Not bad. It's what the Brazilian military and law enforcement use. Want to give it a go?"

"I'd love to."

She led the way out, but did a check of the store before she allowed me to walk from the back room with the rifle. Then we made our way to the shooting range.

It only took me a few minutes to site it in. I was pleased with the way it felt in my hands and it was a nice change to have the kick jolting my shoulder after shooting the laser guns for a month. The one thing I hadn't missed was the loud pop that came with shooting. Even with the ear protection my ears were ringing a bit.

"Do you have a suppressor?"

"Of course. Is this rifle going to be acceptable?"

"Yes, thank you."

She added a suppressor to the transaction and I picked out a set of binoculars and hunting knife before I paid her in cash.

On the drive toward Flores' office building I went over my plans in my mind several times. It was possible I could complete this today and be on my way back home in just a few short hours.

I found a parking garage a couple blocks away and paid to park for the entire day. It didn't take me long to locate Flores' car and I parked a few spaces away. Across the street from the office building was a large park in which I took up residence. A bench afforded me a view directly into Flores' office if I peered through a tree.

The location was perfect. It provided me the excuse of bird and squirrel watching as well as picture taking. The only thing I wished was that the shade from the tree would reach my bench. Within minutes I felt like I was boiling in the sun with sweat dripping into my eyes and off my nose.

Several times I swiveled around on my bench, trying to find a place to set up and take him in his office. Only a couple of the surrounding buildings had a good line of sight but all of them were bustling with people. My presence would be noticed. I didn't think I'd have much trouble getting away before the authorities showed up, but it might be cutting it close, not to mention I'd have to dispose of the rifle somewhere and hope no one could describe me. That wasn't an option for Penumbra.

I wiped the sweat from my face and continued to watch and wait. The park was full of lush vegetation with gorgeous flowers. I decided to take advantage of my waiting time and get some pictures of the flora and fauna as well as the surrounding cityscape. It was certainly a beautiful area.

Though I was playing tourist, I kept an eye on Flores in his office and eventually he left. I didn't know where he'd gone and this worried me some. He could be using the restroom or could be flying off to the wilds. All I could do was wait for him to return or night to fall.

Before long I watched him walk through the main doors of the building. His current path had him coming directly toward me. I went back to my camera and fiddled with it instead of watching him. When I looked up again, Flores had taken a seat at a nearby picnic table and was eating lunch.

The picnic table was slightly behind me off my right shoulder, so it was hard to watch him without turning my head. Using my camera helped immensely. It gave me an excuse to turn in my seat from time to time to keep tabs on Flores. Eventually, he made his way back to the office building. The rest of his day seemed to be as boring as my own, but finally I saw him walking down the sidewalk toward the garage.

The sun was threatening to set and then I'd have to leave my perch. He certainly kept long hours, longer hours than the rest of employees of the same building. People had been leaving the office building in an almost steady stream for the past couple hours. The stream had finally stopped more than half an hour before Flores made his appearance. I kept my distance as I made my way to the same destination.

The garage was fully automated so all I had to do was insert my ticket and go through the turn-style to get to my car. Flores was nowhere to be seen when I got to my vehicle, but his car was still in its spot. I had no idea where he could have gone, so I walked straight to my vehicle. I'd wait for a few minutes and if he didn't retrieve his car I'd go to my designated area near his apartment and wait. It seemed as if his apartment was going to be the final solution.

As I put the key in my door lock an arm slipped around my neck and wrenched me backward. I dropped my bag and brought my hands up to my assailants arm.

"Who are you?" The hot breath carried a hint of fear.

"What?" I could barely speak. It felt like he was crushing my windpipe.

"You've been sitting in the park all day, watching me. Who are you?"

"Just a tourist," I squeaked.

I could have gotten away easily, but chose to go with the ruse until I was sure of my next move.

I heard a gun cock as it pushed into my right side. I kicked myself for allowing this to go further. This was a game-changer and put Flores more in charge than he had been before.

"I'm going to let go and take a look in that bag. Don't make a move or I'll shoot you."

It all seemed to happen at once. He loosened his grip on my neck and pushed at the same time. I felt myself falling forward and wasn't able to regain my balance before I hit the ground. I skinned my knee.

"Ow. You didn't have to push me."

He leveled his gun at my head.

"Open it wide." He nodded toward the bag.

I followed his instructions and watched as his eyes widened at the sight of the rifle.

"Who the hell are you?" He shook his own gun at me.

I gave him a wide, innocent look. "I've got my papers in the bag. Can I get them?"

"Don't touch that gun." His hands were shaking.

I held the bag open wide so he could watch me pluck out the smallish manila envelope I'd been carrying with me. I tried to give it to him.

"Open it!" He ordered. I complied and pulled the Penumbra calling card from the envelope and handed it to him.

"What is this? Is this a joke?" The color had drained from his face as he held the card.

"No, Señor Flores. Not a joke."

I lunged at him.

My intention was to disarm him and finish the job. I didn't want to use his gun because it would draw too much attention and who knew how many more people would be coming in to retrieve their cars. I managed the disarming in quick order, but he fought back and he fought well. There was a decided difference between sparring with a partner and fighting with a man who knew he was fighting for his life. The hair pulling was the worst part until he hit me with a nice punch to the face.

This stunned me a bit and he tried to take his gun back as I shook it off. I grabbed the wrist of his hand that held the gun and snapped it. He screamed and I pushed out and up with my hand, shoving the cartilage from his nose up into his brain. His scream was cut short and his body stiffened. Flores fell backward, legs and arms straight. Almost as soon as he hit the ground I grabbed him under his arms and drug him to his own car. I didn't want any of his blood to pool near my parking spot. I double and triple checked for a pulse before I went back to my own vehicle, and grabbed up the small envelope. I brought it back to Flores' side and shook the contents out onto his still body. Breathing in deeply I inspected my clothes and hands for traces of blood. Somehow I'd managed to keep clean. I reclaimed my bag, shoved it into my car and drove away.

As I drove I reflected on how this turned out. I'd have to be more careful. Though I finished the job, it could have been much worse. It hadn't been perfect and that gnawed at me. There was no excuse for anything other than perfection, especially on a Penumbra job.

I slowed my car enough to chuck the rifle and knife over some bridge and continued to the airport. I wondered if I should have gone back and checked out of the hotel. At least I hadn't left anything in the room, I thought as I finally boarded my flight home.

CLOSE TO FOUR IN THE morning I neared the offices of White and Associates. It was good to get back, but I knew I'd have to lay low for at least a week. I'd gotten myself sunburned as well as a nice black eye. I didn't have any idea how I'd explain any of it to anyone.

I assumed I'd walk into a quiet building but I called White anyway, just to be certain.

"Hello?" His voice was tired as he answered his phone.

"Hey. I'm almost home."

"That was quick." His voice had lost all signs of drowsiness.

"It wasn't as smooth as I'd hoped. Can you meet me in the lobby? I have to make sure no one sees me come in."

"Absolutely. I'll be right down." I heard him struggling and pictured him trying to pull on his pants while he held the phone with his chin to his shoulder.

"I'm still probably ten minutes out."

"See you then." He hung up.

The cab dropped me off outside the building and I walked into the lobby with my head down. I glanced up to see White talking with the guard. As soon as he saw me he hurried to my side.

"What the hell happened?" He put his hand to my chin and lifted my head. He grimaced as he took in my face.

"Let's get to your apartment. Black could be coming down any time now." I put my head back down.

"No." White took my bag for me. "He and Blue are out of town. I sent them back to Wyoming to do another class. They left yesterday afternoon."

"I'd still be more comfortable in your apartment or mine."

"Okay." He took my hand and led me to the elevator. "Yours or mine?" His finger hovered over the buttons.

"Mine, please."

He pushed the button for the twelfth floor. After the doors closed he leaned in toward me and lightly moved my hair away from my black eye.

We rode up to my apartment in silence. White held the doors as I exited the elevators. Once we were at my door he pulled out my key and put it in the lock.

"You okay?" he asked.

"Yes." I nodded for emphasis.

Once we stepped into my apartment he set my bag down and did another inspection of my face and neck.

"I guess I better learn how to put makeup on," I said.

"What happened?" He went to my kitchen and started a pot of coffee.

I went into debriefing mode and gave him all the details.

"Slick," he said when I finished.

"Slick? I completely screwed up."

"No. You did just fine. You got the job done and got out of there."

I pointed to my face. "But how do I explain this? And, I'm sunburned," I whined.

"And you've got a nice bruise on your neck," he added.

"I do?" I walked to my bathroom and inspected my neck.

Sure enough, he'd bruised me there, too. I started rounding up all of my makeup. While I dabbed on the foundation White came up behind me and kissed the back of my neck.

"You're going to make me smear it," I berated him half-heartedly.

"I'm glad you're home." He'd stopped kissing and ran his soft lips from my collarbone to my ear. His hot breath on my neck made my knees want to buckle. Instead I held onto the glass makeup jar hard enough I thought I might break it.

A picture of broken glass embedded in my hand entered my mind, so I reflexively let go of the jar. It clattered into the sink. I was more worried about it killing the mood than whether or not I'd need stitches.

White's soft movements didn't slow with the harsh sound and I turned to face him. He pulled me in close and our lips connected in a hard kiss. It was awkward, but we managed to stay in an embrace all the way to my bedroom where we fell together onto the bed.

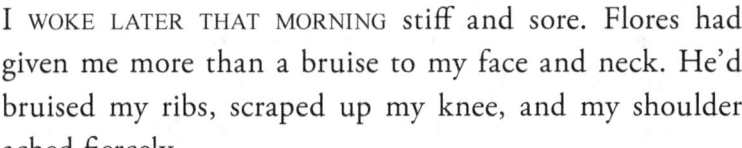

I WOKE LATER THAT MORNING stiff and sore. Flores had given me more than a bruise to my face and neck. He'd bruised my ribs, scraped up my knee, and my shoulder ached fiercely.

White wasn't lying next to me, as expected. I grunted as I rolled out of bed and hobbled into the kitchen. A full pot of coffee called to me and I found a note on the counter under my cup. White had written he was sorry to leave, but he had to get to work and he'd call me later.

I sighed, tossed the note into the trash, and poured my coffee. The heat and aroma were soothing and I considered relaxing at my kitchen bar for at least one full cup. The sting from the sunburn changed my mind.

After I slathered on the lotion I'd gotten from Scott for sunburns I went back to my coffee pot and refreshed my cup.

Again the call of the barstool was strong, but my computer chair was more comfortable. I went to my bag, pulled out my camera, and spent the morning playing around with the photos I'd taken in Lima.

I replayed the job over in my head several times. When did he realize I was watching him? Where should I have done the hit? I should have stayed undercover at all times. I had been bold and relied on my ability to blend in for too long of a period. Finally, I closed out my photo program and searched for Lima headlines on the Internet. It didn't take long to find the one I was looking for. Penumbra had struck again. This time, he'd taken one of Lima's finest, except it had just recently come to light that the victim was suspected of taking bribes. There was no mention of any evidence being found other than the routine calling card.

I was considering calling out for lunch when my phone rang "How're you feeling? Did you get enough sleep?"

"I'm a little sore, but I'm fine."

"From the looks of the rest of your body, you're lucky you got out of there." He sighed. "What do you think of telling people that someone tried to mug you?"

"That works, but how do I explain the sunburn?"

"I don't know. That one's harder. How about you tried out a tanning bed and stayed in too long?"

"I suppose that could work. Okay. That's the story. I went tanning, stayed in too long and then got mugged on the way home. You should see the other guy."

White's laugh was brief. "You'll be leaving for EOD and flight training later today."

"Today? I just got back," I grumbled. "I hoped to spend more time with you."

"I know, but Brown wants to get it over with."

"Fine." I decided not to argue. Brown wasn't the only one who wanted to get this over with.

"Now that we've got that out of the way, would you like to come down for lunch?"

"I'd love to."

"Hurry. Our food is already getting cold."

I did the best I could with my makeup but decided I needed a lot more practice when I inspected my job. I washed it off and tried to just blend away the bruises on my face and neck. It didn't work well with the sunburn so I washed my face again and decided to carry the bruises with pride.

As I rode the elevator down it stopped on Red's floor.

"Damn it," I said before the doors opened.

"Ms. Grey," Red greeted me as he stepped on and turned to face the doors. He didn't seem to notice my wounds.

He held the doors for me as I stepped out onto the seventh floor.

"So? What happened to your face and neck?" he asked as he followed close behind me.

I didn't answer him until I stepped into the outer office. Gabriella would want the story. Her expression was just as I expected, a mix of fear and concern. "Some guy tried to mug me," I said.

"Are you okay, hon?" She stood from her chair.

"I'm fine, Gabriella. I'm here to see White."

"Does he know?" She indicated my appearance her face contorted with anger.

"Yes. It's okay. I'm okay. He's expecting me."

"Of course. And you, too?" she asked Red.

"Yes, please."

Damn it. I can't get ten minutes with White anymore. Maybe Red will get out quickly.

Gabriella pushed the intercom button. "Ms. Grey and Mr. Red are here to see you."

"Send them in." White's voice was unreadable.

Red allowed me to lead him into the office and took the seat to my left.

"Sorry, Red," White said as he handed me the white Styrofoam box that held my lunch. "If I'd have known you were coming down I would have ordered you something. What can I do for you?"

"Actually, I was just coming down to ask you where Ms. Grey was when we met on the elevator." He hiked his head toward me.

"Me? What did you need?" I asked.

"Nothing. I just haven't seen you around for a couple days. I was just wondering where you were."

"Oh, I've been hanging out in my apartment." I shrugged.

The three of us sat in silence for a couple of minutes as White and I ate our lunch. Finally, White said, "I called you down to let you know that you'll be leaving for EOD and flight training early this evening."

"Sounds good," I said with a full mouth. "Where am I going?" I played along.

"Nevada. Brown is teaching the EOD class and I've gotten Will to do the flight training. Do you think you can handle both classes at the same time?"

"I think so." Again, the three of us sat in silence as White and I ate. White showed no signs of concern but I was uncomfortable. Finally, I offered Red some of my food.

"No thanks. I already had lunch."

"I think you'll enjoy this training," White said.

"I know I'll enjoy the flight training." I grinned at the thought.

"EOD is probably more important than the flight training," Red said.

The ice had been broken and the three of us chatted and my uncomfortable feeling passed. Red remained through the meal and stayed even after I left to go pack for my four-month fiesta. He either had something to talk to White about that he didn't want me to hear or he was just being an ass and making sure we'd have no time alone. I suspected the latter.

Red seemed sure of my relationship status with White and I didn't expect him to let it drop until we admitted it. I still wasn't sure if we should admit it or keep it secret, but I didn't know how long I could take this extra attention from Red.

Brown showed up at my apartment a few short hours later. I was packed but I wasn't ready to leave. Of course, I had to explain my bruises and sun burn again.

"I hope you kicked his ass," Brown said after I told him I'd been mugged.

"I don't think he's in very good shape today."

"Did you report it?"

"No. He didn't get anything and he ran away."

"He was still able to run away? What the hell were you thinking? You should have broken his legs."

I laughed. "I broke his nose."

"At least you broke something."

We arrived at the Nevada compound late that evening and went to the compound bar for a couple drinks.

Brown said, "We won't start training for a couple days. We might as well relax and have a little fun before we have to work."

Chapter Fourteen

"BROWN INFORMED ME THIS IS our last morning in the simulator." Will's regret was obvious, even through the headphones.

I sighed into the microphone. "I know. I finished EOD yesterday." The four months had not passed quickly and had been full of hardships for me. For one thing, I hated EOD. White hadn't contacted me once while I'd been in Nevada. Also, I'd realized I enjoyed Will's voice in my ear much more than I wanted to. The first month had been okay, but no contact with White had killed my spirit. I still held hope, but doubt had grown roots and would soon start producing fruit or berries or melons. Whatever it was that doubt produced once it was mature.

Flight training and getting to know White's little brother better had been the only reason I was able to complete Explosive Ordinance Disposal.

As my feelings for Will grew so did my guilt and longing for White. The old adage *out of sight, out of mind* , popped up almost every day as my thoughts inevitably wandered to White. Why couldn't the saying be right? Decisions and conversations would be much easier if I could just get White out of my mind. I was convinced he'd forgotten about me.

The similarities between the brothers didn't help, either. Every day Will would say something that reminded me of White, but he did have his own way with things, too. For one thing, he was much more open in our conversations than White had ever been. This made it easier for me to be more candid with him and as a result, we'd developed a real connection.

Even though Will was back home and I was at the Nevada compound, the mornings I'd spent with him had made me appreciate him as more than just White's cute little brother. My guilt was thick but I knew it would be worse had he been training me in person.

"Brown told me you did great with EOD. You've done great with flight training, too. As soon as we get a chance I'll take you up in one of the jets. This time you'll have the controls all to yourself and Brown will have no say." His voice had perked up and invaded my pining.

Butterflies fluttered around in my stomach. Mostly in anticipation of flying the real thing instead of the simulator, but partly at the thought of spending time with Will. I hated myself for feeling this way, but White's absence over the past four months really bothered me and Will was the closest thing to White I'd had. I knew there could never be anything solid between us, but I couldn't help wondering *what if*.

"Rick told me you should be home this afternoon." Will rarely referred to his brother by his alias, Mr. White.

"When did you talk to Rick?" I fought a quiver at the mention of White's name.

"Oh, I've been going to the office almost every day since you started training with me. He asked me to keep him up to date on your progress."

White wasn't completely ignoring me. Actually he was ignoring *me* but he wasn't ignoring my training.

"He hasn't contacted me at all since I started EOD."

"He wouldn't. You're in training."

"He always has before. Plus, Brown lets me talk to you."

"You've been talking to me because I've been involved in your training this time around."

"I suppose."

I didn't completely believe Will. Deep down I still wanted White, but I was afraid it was probably one of those things that would remain forever in the background. Besides, the *what if* was a little fun to think about.

The conversation turned, as it usually did, to what we were supposed to be doing in the simulator – flight training. The time allotted for our session expired too quickly. We exchanged glum goodbyes and promised to get together as soon as I got home.

"I THOUGHT YOU WERE GOING to be in there all day." Brown startled me as I stepped out of the simulator.

I caught myself just before I toppled backward. "I didn't expect to see you here, you sneak."

Brown laughed. "I don't know about you, but I'm ready to get home. I packed for you." He held out my large duffle bag.

"You didn't snoop through my stuff, did you?" I grabbed at it.

"Of course I did. You're boring. Did you know that?"

"Jackass." I replied and I meant it. Brown and I acted like siblings, but I was acutely aware that he was not my brother. The last thing I wanted him doing was touching my underwear.

We made our way to the chopper that Brown had ready to go. I thought he'd let me fly, at least part of the way home, but he wouldn't let me touch the controls.

"Why won't you let me fly?" I complained more than halfway through the flight.

"Because, you've spent the last four months in the simulator and I haven't been able to fly anything. I've been grounded because you needed EOD training."

I had always wanted to learn to fly but I didn't realize my passion until Will took me up in the jet so many months ago.

The main thing the two of us had in common were the stars in our eyes whenever we even thought of flying. Until now, it never occurred to me Brown must have the same feelings. Though my fingers itched to take the controls, I understood his need and decided to be content just to be up in the air.

As we neared the office building that housed White & Associates and our apartments the palms of my hands started to sweat. I wiped them on my pant legs as inconspicuously as possible.

"Should I check in at the office?"

I had mixed feelings about this. I'd been okay with no contact for the first month of training but then I really started to worry. Three months of wondering where I stood with White had put a strain on me and I dreaded all outcomes. If White had gotten over me and only wanted a professional relationship I would be heartbroken. Yet, if he was happy to see me and wanted to pick up where we left off, did I?

"I have to go give your final progress report so you'd have to wait, anyway. I'm sure White can find you if he needs to." Brown set the chopper down smoothly.

"I guess I'll be in my apartment if anyone needs me."

I TOSSED MY DUFFLE INTO the corner and headed to my computer. My computer was always what I missed the most when I went off for any kind of training. At least that's what I thought I missed the most for the first five minutes. Time slowed to a crawl as my eyes wandered back and forth from my computer screen to my phone. *Is he going to call?*

A knock on my door made me jump in my seat. I straightened my shirt and my hair and answered it.

"Glad you're home." Black stood in my doorway with a grin.

I was only slightly disappointed when he walked past me into my apartment.

"I'm glad to be home."

"Brown and Will just briefed the rest of us on your progress. Sounds like you did as I expected."

"EOD sucks, but the flight instruction kept me going. So, what's been going on?"

"Not much. Small jobs that we've been farming out to the employees, nothing needing the involvement of the partners. I should have gone to the cabin." He'd made his way to the coffee pot.

"Sorry. I'll make some." I reached around him and pulled the freezer door open. "Grab the coffee for me." I'd learned after my extended trips the best place to put coffee, so it doesn't go stale, is the freezer.

"Here." Black handed me the cold container.

The two of us sat in comfortable silence enjoying our coffee when a knock came at my door. My heart leaped and again I straightened my hair and shirt before going to answer it.

Black had followed me to the front door.

"Will." Black said as he slid past us and out the door.

Will reached out and shook his hand and turned back to me. "May I come in?"

"Sure." Saying the word was a chore. "See you later," I called to Black as he stepped into the elevator.

"I was in the building and thought it would be terrible if I didn't stop in," Will said.

He'd already found a chair at my kitchen bar.

"I'm glad you did," I said.

My innards were getting quite the workout today.

"Would you like some coffee?" I gestured to the freshly brewed pot.

"Sure."

He was quiet while I poured him a cup but I could feel his eyes on me.

"Thanks." He took the steaming brew I held out for him.

He took a careful sip as I refilled my own cup. The moment became decidedly awkward.

"You realize we've not actually seen each other since we went joy riding in the Goshawk in Nevada?"

I smiled. "Yes. That thought has actually crossed my mind several times." A flash of the memory broadened my smile.

"It's different than talking to a microphone." He indicated our face-to-face conversation with a back and forth motion of his hand. His warm smile invited me in just enough to make me blush. He was definitely a Malone boy.

"Would you like to join me for lunch?" His inviting smile remained and was accompanied by a hopeful hike of his eyebrows. Will's tone of voice didn't waver but I noticed that his coffee cup was shaking in his hands as he set it down.

Is he nervous?

"I'd love to." I splashed coffee as I set my cup down next to his and felt my face growing warmer again.

"Shall we, then?" He rose from his seat and offered his arm. I took it and we quietly rode the elevator to his vehicle in the parking garage.

The tension lifted as he drove us to the restaurant and we talked about my EOD training. He'd not undergone much training for explosives and was genuinely curious, unlike me. It hadn't taken me long to realize it wasn't something I wanted much to do with in the future. However, I humored him and told him all about my training.

Inside the restaurant the conversation changed to various topics, like it usually did during my flight training. We talked about childhood experiences. He told me about the time him and Rick tried to parachute from a rock wall with pillowcases. Rick made him jump first and he almost broke his arm.

The addition of Rick Malone, A.K.A. Mr. White, into our conversation threw me a little. Rick was the last person I wanted to think about while out to lunch with his brother. The reminder that he did exist injected feelings of guilt.

It's just lunch. Besides, Black and Will came to see me, he didn't even call.

After internally berating myself I told the story of the first time I jumped from an airplane with an instructor and then ended with the first time I jumped to the cabin and was pulled into the lake with the parachute. The description of how hard it was to pull that damn thing out of the water made him laugh.

I ate as slowly as I could, hopefully without being obvious, and I noticed Will's pace matched mine. Was it for the same reason or was he just being polite? When I finally finished my sandwich I expected to leave but we sat and visited for an hour more.

Eventually, the looks from the wait staff made me conscious that they probably wanted their table open for new customers. I suggested we had better go and Will left money on the table for our meal and I put some extra on the table. I couldn't go without paying something.

The afternoon sun was warm and my hair hovered in the slight breeze for a second. I waited for Will to reach my side before I stepped into the parking lot.

"Thank you for lunch," I said.

"Do you want to go for a walk?" Will had stopped in the middle of the road and indicated the sidewalk with a shift of his head.

"Sure." I wanted nothing more than to spend more time with Will.

It took us half an hour to cover two blocks to the nearest park where we sat on a bench. I didn't even notice the time until the sun started to set.

"We better get back," I said.

"Would you like a tour of the carrier?"

"The carrier?"

"Yeah. I'm shipping out soon. Someone has to fly the jets off the ship. I thought you might like a tour before I go."

"You're leaving?" I didn't try to hide my disappointment.

"It's a six month tour. But, I'll be back before you know it."

At some point in the day we'd scooted very close together on the bench and I was keenly aware of that fact now as Will leaned toward me. He put a hand on my knee and one on my waist. My breath caught in my throat and before I knew what was happening, his lips were made their way toward mine. I wanted to melt into the kiss. I wanted to be held and loved so why wouldn't my internal voice shut up?

I told myself that this could never work. I followed that up with, *just shut up and enjoy it* . Next came thoughts of where this could actually lead. An internal movie of Will and me involved in some very private actions flitted across my closed eyes followed by White's disapproving look when he found out what we'd been doing.

So what. I should be able to have a relationship with whomever I want to. Obviously, White didn't want me. Then the thought of Penumbra came crashing in and I pulled away before the kiss began.

"What's wrong?" Will asked.

"I'm sorry." I took a deep breath to help stabilize my excess energy. "I can't."

"It's Rick, isn't it." Will sighed.

"Actually, no. Not really. I just— There are things— I know this wouldn't work out in the long run."

I knew I could never tell Will about Penumbra. I wanted to be able to tell him about being Penumbra but it was something I had never even considered doing. Never having considered bringing Will into my inner most secrets was very significant.

"Who cares about the long run? It certainly works for the moment." He tried to pull me in for another kiss but that last statement killed it. The magic was no longer strong enough.

"I've been living in the moment all day and I can't do it. I have to think about the future." I scooted away from him.

Gabriella had told me to feed my libido many times before, but this was too risky. I didn't think White would ever forgive me if I took things too far with his little brother.

He closed the distance I'd put between us. "Why? Why can't we just have a little fun before I ship out?" He reached up and brushed my hair behind my ear.

If there had been any lingering effects of Will's charm it had no chance of ever resurfacing. I should have been seething with rage, but instead, I laughed.

"What?" He looked around as if he'd find the joke somewhere in the fading light.

"Obviously I think you're attractive and boy, do you have the charm, but I can't see this going past friendship. I better get home." I stood from the bench and Will did the same.

"What about the tour?"

"You still want to give me a tour?" I was surprised.

"Sure. Just because you won't sleep with me doesn't mean I don't still like you. I might just like you even more." When I had no immediate response he walked up and put his arm across my shoulders and gave a friendly squeeze. "Come on. You can't blame a guy for trying."

"Yes, I can. But, I won't." I sighed. "I guess I'll take that tour."

"Great. Let's get going, then."

His switch from romance to friendship was immediate and a bit jarring. Will did all the talking back to the car. By the time I buckled in I'd switched gears as well. Strangely enough, our moment might have strengthened our friendship. Now we knew there was nothing more written in the stars for us. I could still think he was as cute as they came but I wouldn't have to wonder *what if*.

Will talked a lot of facts and figures about carriers as we drove. The big numbers all became comprehensible as we pulled into the parking lot across the street. The immensity of the ship was almost overwhelming. The thing was huge.

"No wonder they call them floating cities," I marveled as we walked toward the monstrosity.

We were allowed to board without much ado. Will showed me his berthing in the officer's quarters and introduced me to a few of his friends. I heard them whispering after we left but couldn't pick out what they were saying.

"You'll be the talk of the tour," he admitted.

He led me to the hanger bay and I was surprised not to see any jets. When I asked him about it he said his squadron would fly them onto the ship after deployment. He explained the rush of landing and taking off from a carrier and the description gave me chills.

We eventually found ourselves on the flight deck and he explained in further detail about landing planes on the ship. I was finding everything riveting and was truly lamenting my current occupation.

"Are you hungry?" He asked after checking his watch.

"Actually I'm not." I held my stomach. It had been through a lot today. "But if you are we could still go somewhere," I added.

"It's almost eight thirty. I'll just stop and get some fast food."

Even after all the excitement I'd already had I was disappointed the outing was coming to a close.

He led me off of the carrier and back toward the vehicle.

"I'm not ready to call it a night. Are you?" He asked as the engine roared to life.

"What are you up for?"

"I thought we might go clubbing."

"I'd love to, but—" I struggled to come up with an excuse.

"Don't say no," he pleaded. "If it's because you don't want to piss Rick off. It'll be good for him and I'm sure Brown would be game to chaperone us—"

"White has no bearing on my social life," I said more strongly than I intended. Apparently, the substitution of White for Rick wasn't lost on him because he raised his eyebrows and grinned.

"Then please, don't say no." He narrowed his eyes and his grin became even more wicked. "I was sure your reason for turning me down was Rick, but now I'm really interested."

I struggled with myself for a moment but finally decided to just come out and say it. "I don't take sex lightly."

"You're a strong woman. I find it hard to believe you'd repress that part of yourself."

"It's not repression, it's—discretion."

"Well, Miss Prude, we could still go get Brown to protect your reputation, but then again, who'd talk about us if we did?" His expression and body language screamed White but he had a healthy dose of Brown's influence coursing through his veins.

"Let 'em talk," I said.

"I knew I liked you."

"Let's do it." I put on my own evil grin.

We drove in silence for a few blocks before Will spoke.

"Alex." His brow furrowed. "I don't know what your life plans are but I do know what mine are. Even though I led you to believe I live only in the moment. I plan to get a little further in my career and then settle down. I want to get married and have some kids. I may or may not stay in the Navy." He paused and took his gaze away from the road for a moment.

I was too afraid of what was coming next to breathe.

"Anyway." He returned his attention back to his driving. "You could fit into that scenario very easily. But, I know how Rick feels about you. We have a long-standing competition when it comes to women and I didn't realize how serious he was until today. I could never do anything to hurt my brother. We've talked about you and I've promised to lay off until you make up your mind about him. I'm kind of breaking the rules right now though." He laughed uncomfortably. My jaw worked, trying to make words, but speaking requires air and I still had none.

He added quickly. "I'm not asking you any questions right now, so don't think you have to give any answers. Besides, I'm out to sea for six months this time around and a lot can happen in six months. Maybe—"

My mind raced and I blurted out, "I haven't told Rick that I love him." I was horrified at myself, but the damage was already done. "I don't see anything coming of it, but..."

"I was afraid of that. Even if you didn't love him, it'd be a struggle for us because of his feelings for you."

I took a shaky breath. "I'm sorry, Will. If I had met you first—"

"No need to be sorry. Though you and I are compatible I do think you and Rick are more compatible."

"I wouldn't be so sure. He shipped me off for EOD for four months and still hasn't contacted me. That doesn't sound like he has much in the way of feelings for me, but I'm okay with it." The lump in my throat grew.

I didn't dare let my hopes climb from Will's admission of White's feelings. Yet, Will should know his brother's mind, right? Especially since they'd recently talked about me. Then again, even if White did love me, and the moments I'd given him hadn't been just a fling, he had a bad way of showing it.

"Just don't tell him what I told you." I pushed the lump down. I would not allow White to get the best of me if he'd just used me.

"I wondered how sincere he was. At least, I did until I spent a day with you. There is no way he's not completely committed."

"Will. He's the boss of the company. If he'd wanted to contact me, he would have. Hell, he could have flown out to see me. But, he didn't." I tried to force the sorrow to change to anger. "I pictured myself growing old with Rick, but my current life choice doesn't allow for growing old or any of the regular stuff that goes with that."

Conversation ceased while Will ordered a burger and fries at the nearest drive up window. I allowed him to eat in silence while I contemplated White's inattention once again.

To begin the night inside my comfort zone we went to the Skylight first. I'd done my fair share of partying in the past but I'd only been to a few select bars. Anthony, my one and only ex-boyfriend, was bartending and Will made sure to point him out to me.

"How did you know about Anthony?"

"Rick told me." He shrugged.

"You two make a habit of talking about my past?"

It was a bit flattering that the two men I found the most attractive and appealing would be discussing my love life. However, since my escapades consisted of just Anthony it was more embarrassing than flattering.

"No. There's not much history to talk about. I think we covered it all in one or two conversations." He winked.

I was startled and embarrassed so I just shook my head in disapproval.

"Let's go say hi to Anthony. Rick also told me a few things about Anthony that I bet you don't even know." Will raised his brow in a challenge that I left unanswered. I was too engrossed in my thoughts anyway.

We made our way to the bar, Will hanging back a little. True to form, Anthony came right to me.

"Wow. I thought you'd moved. I haven't seen you forever. How long has it been? A year?"

He did his best to show off his severely lacking biceps by imitating *The Thinker*. Actually, they didn't look half bad but I knew he didn't know how to use them, so they didn't count.

"Nope. Didn't move. Can you get me a coke and—" I turned to get Will's order but Anthony cut in, true to form and oblivious.

"I'm glad you came to see me. I'm currently between girlfriends." He waggled his eyebrows at me.

"I'm currently taken."

What happened next I didn't expect. Will stepped out from behind me and Anthony visibly paled.

"Ssss—sorry," he stuttered. "I didn't mean anything by it. Please tell Malone not to— not to—"

"Don't worry, Anthony. She's on *my* arm tonight, not my brother's. Can you please get the lady her coke and add a beer and two shots of whiskey."

"On the house." Anthony quickly filled our order and busied himself with another customer.

"What was that all about? Black didn't even intimidate him that much."

"Rick told me about a visit he paid to Anthony a while ago. Good to know he hasn't forgotten."

"When did— What did he do?" Will ignored me and led me away from the bar to a table near the dance floor.

We each had a couple of drinks and danced to a few songs before we decided it was time to move onto the next bar. By the time we were leaving the third bar on the list I was ready to call it a night. Will, on the other hand, was just getting started. I told him I had to slow down on the drinking and he complied by ordering me a coke at bar number four. I was thankful because I was surprised I could even remember I'd already had five shots. It had been months since I'd had any alcohol and I'd never been able to handle it well anyway.

Bar number five could have been The Rave as far as I was concerned. The deep tones radiating through my body sent me to places I hadn't been for a long time. Penumbra had finally gone to sleep, taking with her Ms. Grey leaving just Alex to enjoy the climate.

The dance floor looked like a very shallow swimming pool, surrounded by railings. Will and I found an opening near the railing after I declined his offer to dance. Instead, I held on to the railing, closed my eyes, let go of all thought, and swayed with the reverberations. The feel of the close bodies, the sounds that evolved into vibrations shaking me to the core, the scents of too much or too little perfume around me. About half and hour later a very distinctive aroma snuck in on my consciousness and brought me back to reality.

Will stood to my left wearing a smile but seemingly much more aware than I had been. I looked around for the source of the smell and was rewarded with White right behind me wearing his indecipherable look.

"What are you doing here?" Having to yell didn't help mask the slur in my voice.

White was the last person I wanted to see right now. The urge to say something fueled by my drunken state was very strong. I had to resist. Only a moment ago nothing but the vibrations from the music existed for me and now I was confronted with my biggest problem. It could go either way if I decided to interact with White right now. I had no idea if I'd punch him dead in the face or reach up and kiss him.

White hiked his head toward Will.

"I'm out of money and I know better than to drive at this point." Will swayed as if to emphasize the fact that he shouldn't be driving.

"I would have paid for a cab." I yelled.

"I'm not asking a girl to pay on a date." The shock on his face emphasized the concept was obviously unthinkable.

White mirrored Will's shrug, giving me déjà vu. I looked back to Will and he grinned and winked at me. They were going to give me whiplash.

I leaned in to talk in Will's ear. "I thought you wanted to give the guys something to talk about."

I'd been looking forward to making White wonder if Will and I got along extra well and now I didn't know how to go about it without actually doing something drastic.

"Oh, they've already started," he returned into my ear.

His voice in my ear gave me chills and made me giggle like a girl. I'm sure the alcohol helped. It didn't take me long to get lost in the music again. Strangely enough it was even easier to lose myself with White directly behind me. I knew I'd be safe with these two men near and I was able to relax.

The strength of the music finally released its hold long enough for me to realize I'd backed up enough to just feel White's heat against my back. I don't know how long I'd been that close to him but I knew it was time to go home or my uninhibited state would get the better of me. I turned my head just enough to get a glimpse of White's face. He was scanned the crowd and, like at The Rave, there was a small bubble around us as he held Will and I under his protection. White must have felt my eyes on him because he looked down at me. I mouthed the words, "Are you ready to go?" and he answered with a nod of his head.

I got Will's attention and asked him the same thing in a shout. He also nodded his agreement.

I CHOSE TO SIT IN the back of White's black Mustang, though the backseat was extremely uncomfortable. But I figured I'd be left out of the conversation on the way home if I did and they didn't let me down. I'd definitely had too much to drink and didn't need to emphasize that fact with my slurred speech.

Will generously helped me navigate my way out of the vehicle once we'd parked in the garage of White and Associates. I held my own quite well after I got to my feet and Will and White let me lead the way into the lobby where I was greeted by all of my partners. Green and Black sported disapproving looks but Red, Blue and especially Brown all wore broad smiles.

"Pay up." Will stumbled up to Brown with his hand out.

"I want proof first. So, Ms. Grey. Did you have a good time tonight?"

I guardedly nodded my answer. He took a swing at me and I had him on the floor instantly but I didn't brace myself and the momentum pulled me down on top of him. We were face to face on the ground, staring eye to eye. I was well aware of how this looked so I scrambled to get up. Brown let out a laugh and stood, lifting me easily as he rose. He made sure I was steady on my feet before he let go of my waist.

"Okay. Here you go." He pulled out a wad of cash. Money passed between everyone and I had no idea what was going on.

White was the only one not handing out or receiving cash. I gave him a questioning look then slurred, "What's going on?"

"Will bet the guys he could take you out and get you drunk."

"What!"

White gave me his evil grin, the one that tied me in knots. I stammered, "I didn't mean to get drunk." I redirected my fury at Will.

"What the hell?" The slur was almost gone.

"I was going to win one way or another, tonight." He shrugged.

Again, I should have been livid but one look at White and his smug look of satisfaction doused the flames. Will just admitted in front of my partners that I wouldn't allow him into my bed. Then another thought overtook everything else. I swiveled and poked White hard in the chest. "Did the two of you plan this?" I was mortified that this might be a test. If Will would have been able to get me into bed, then I wasn't really the girl for his brother.

Will stepped between us and pulled me to the side. "He had no idea I took you out today." He was tried to be low-key but I was sure everyone could hear his loud whispers. "He has no idea we spent the whole day together. He didn't even know we were together until I called him for a ride."

"Will they still let you ship out if you have a black eye?" I glared.

"Why wouldn't they?" He wore a confused look.

I'm sure the revelation of what I meant hit him when my fist did, but maybe not until he hit the floor. When he looked up at me while cupping his hand over the offended eye I offered my hand. My partners all laughed at him and he finally donned a huge grin and took my hand.

"I'll take you home." White had his hands on my elbows, ready to usher me off and out of danger, but we were instantly swarmed by the rest of the men with Brown up front.

"Oh no you don't! You, Black and Blue are the only guys that have been around her when her tongue has been loosened by spirits. The rest of us want to get to know our partner like we know each other."

"No, no, no. I think White's right and I should go home." I protested as Brown wiggled his way between White and me and pushed me toward the elevator.

I looked back at White for help but he was lost in the sea of men following behind us. I'd had visions of White and I in my apartment and me making some verbal and physical statements I could never take back. Whiskey was a great spine strengthener.

Everyone piled into the elevator and I felt a little claustrophobic. The feeling came mostly from everyone poking fun at me and Will rather than the closeness of the bodies. When the doors opened I pushed my way out to a floor I'd never been on before.

"Where are we?" I asked as Red pushed past me.

"Welcome to my abode," he said.

He threw open the door and showcased the interior with a flourish of his arm. I walked in and was overwhelmed with the feel of it.

"Now this is exactly what I thought White's apartment would look like."

The black and red accents made me think of Gigi's, the strip joint that Colin had me working at before the Dimitri hit.

Black let out a chuckle as he followed me inside.

All of our apartments were the same floor plan but we each had a room that we used for our personal touch. White's housed C.I.C., mine remained unoccupied with anything but storage items. Black's housed plants and all kinds of non-bachelor items and Red's was set up as a game room. He had a bar in one corner, a pool table, a dart board, and those tall tables that only seated a couple of people. However, he did have a couple of larger tables that would allow us all to sit together.

Blue stepped behind the bar and brought back ice wrapped in a towel.

"Let me look at that." Blue tipped Will's head back and examined his nicely reddening eye. "I don't think it'll affect your ability to fly." He pressed the towel into Will's hands with instructions to put it on his eye.

Brown started pouring shots like a pro and didn't even ask any of us what we wanted. Because of this I assumed he wasn't making one for me but I was mistaken. He brought over my usual shot with a coke back.

"I can't drink this," I said as I pushed the shot away.

"Gonna be sick?" Brown teased.

"Not yet, but I might soon." I stuck my tongue out at him.

"Oh, come on. You're home now. Who cares if you get sick. Just as long as you make it to the bathroom," Red added.

"I promise to hold your hair." Brown pushed the shot closer to me.

Eventually the prodding got to me and I threw back my shot with the rest of them. After the first one they didn't offer me anymore.

Their drinking continued but after a couple more I took my leave, followed closely by White.

"I really had no intentions of getting drunk," I told him again.

"I know. I'll make sure you get to your apartment." He led me by the elbow to the elevator, off of the elevator and straight into my apartment.

"I'm sorry," I blurted out.

"No need to be. I know Will can be very persuasive when he wants to be. A couple of drinks isn't a big deal."

As we stood near the door my guilt was intense but the urge to kiss him was almost overwhelming. I wanted to scream at him that I'd almost kissed his brother but I couldn't deal with how he might take it. I felt like I'd cheated on White. As soon as I'd seen him standing behind me at the bar I knew that all of the inattention hadn't mattered. I was his and he was mine, forever.

"So, you were out with him all day?" His eyes narrowed some.

"He asked me to lunch and the time flew by. Then he gave me a tour of the carrier." I found myself looking at the floor as I described my day in as few words as possible.

"I see." I looked up in time to see the regret on White's face as he said, "I should get going. Will defended your honor in the lobby and there's no reason I should screw that up. Besides, I'm missing all the fun. I'm sure the guys are really laying it on thick now that you're gone."

My heart dropped. What if Will told them that we almost shared a kiss? How could I explain that to Rick?

"I'm sorry," I said again. The guilt of spending the day with Will before even trying to contact White on my own was eating at me.

"It's okay." His sad smile and soft touch to my cheek wrenched at me. "Like I said, Will can be very persuasive."

He left me standing there wondering what I'd just admitted to.

Chapter Fifteen

WHEN I WOKE THE NEXT morning I was afraid to open my eyes. The headache was sure to be there. As I lay there, trying to decide if my stomach felt queasy, the full memory of the previous day, the almost-kiss with Will, and White softly dismissing me with sorrow on his face, made me sit straight up.

The headache and the queasy feeling were overwhelming and sent me running to the bathroom where I sat on the cold tile until the feeling passed.

I filled the sink with cold water, bent over and dunked my head in.

Maybe he doesn't know for sure that Will tried to kiss me.

I considered taking in a deep breath while under water. Instead, I held my breath for as long as I could then drained the water and brushed my teeth.

The hangover subsided as I showered. Almost like I was washing it down the drain. But, what I really needed was some food and I didn't have anything acceptable in my cupboards.

I briefly considered calling Black, my usual morning company, but needed some female companionship.

I had overslept and taken my time in the shower so I knew Gabriella would already be in the office. That meant it was either her company or breakfast. I couldn't have both.

To hell with it. Maybe I can talk White into letting her come to breakfast with me.

I wasn't looking forward to seeing him right now, yet I really wanted to know how he'd treat me, now that we were both sober.

My heart beat heavily as I forced myself out of my apartment and into the elevator.

Gabriella was at her desk as I suspected and jumped to her feet when I walked in.

She let out a jovial, "Hey!" making me wince.

Rounding the corner of her desk she pulled my face into her hands and looked me over.

"You look a little green, but you healed up nicely from your mugging."

"Had several too many last night."

"Ahh—" She smiled and resumed her position behind her desk.

"Do you think White would let you go out for breakfast with me?" I pointed to his closed office door.

"Probably not since he isn't here yet. Your late night have anything to do with his?" Her eyebrows wagged up and down.

"Kind of, just not in the way you are suggesting." I sighed.

"Everything okay, hon?"

"Yeah. I just wanted to talk. You know, girl time."

"We can talk now," she offered.

"I have to get something to eat before the hangover has a chance to regain its fury."

"That bad, huh?"

I nodded.

"You better eat, then. We can talk later."

MY PUKE GREEN MUSTANG WAS in its spot in the garage. It felt good to slide behind the wheel of my favorite possession.

I chose a quiet little restaurant and had a very quiet breakfast before I took a quiet drive around the city.

Though I'd felt mostly alone for the past four months I realized now that I had never been alone. I found it refreshing to be out on my own again. The only drawback was that my mind would not shut up about Will and White.

After more than an hour of driving aimlessly and dwelling on nothing but White I decided to just ignore my worry. What was done was done and even if White never spoke to me again I would not actually die. Even if I wanted to, I wouldn't. There was no point in going over it in my mind for eternity.

Eventually, my car found its way to my parent's place. I almost drove back to the guesthouse from habit, but parked in the front drive instead.

When I reached the front door I hesitated. Should I ring the bell? Should I just walk in like I still lived here? I felt a little out of place so I opted for the ring the bell approach.

No one was answering. I debated on whether I should leave or try the door when my mother appeared.

"Alex. You're home." She pulled me into a tight embrace.

"Hi, Mom." I managed after she released me.

"Get in here."

She beamed as she pulled me across the threshold and walked in the direction of the kitchen. My nose picked up so many different aromas I had trouble separating them. I thought I detected lavender for a fleeting second and just as quickly I smelled something minty. The scents overwhelmed me and I gave up trying to figure out what they were.

I took a seat at the kitchen table that was covered with metal tubes and various powders and vials of liquid.

"What's all this?" I picked up a small glass container labeled Eucalyptus Oil.

"I've decided to make my own candles and bath salts. I even make shampoo and lotion." She brought over a plastic bottle of what I assumed was lotion.

"Try it." She pushed the bottle into my hands.

I lifted the bottle to my nose and was pleased with the smell.

"What scent is this?" Having it close to my face helped to single out the aroma against all the others in the air. It was fresh and clean smelling.

"Cucumber melon. I thought you'd like that one. You can have it."

As I put some on my hands and started to rub it in she started firing off her questions about what I'd been doing.

I filled her in on everything I did for EOD and flight training and she surprised me with some of the technical questions she asked.

I knew that she had left the Penumbra legacy to me, but we had never talked shop all that much. Every time we did I felt strange. There was this huge part of my mother I never knew existed. I had always thought her main role in life was to cook dinner and satisfy her curiosity with domestic hobbies like making candles and lotions and even taking the danger up a notch and working with power tools. It was always surprising that my mother knew so much about my chosen profession.

"Any *jobs* lately?" she finally asked.

"No. I've been out of touch because of the training and if there were any offers White didn't bring them to my attention."

Her question brought me back to Lima for a brief moment. I wanted to tell her what happened, but I worried she might wonder if I was the right person for the job. White had told me all was fine, but I knew I'd screwed up in Lima. Flores had seen me, attacked me and even hurt me. It took me a couple weeks to get back to my normal self. Then I was brought back even further to the day I asked White how often I might expect to get Penumbra jobs. Was it normal to go months without a contract?

"Is that unusual?" I asked.

"No. Why do you think I do stuff like this?" She gestured toward the cluttered table. "I had to find something to occupy my time. At least you have White and Associates and on the job training to keep you busy. What I wouldn't have given to have had your distractions."

"I'm not so sure you'd want my distractions." My mind went directly to White. "At least you've always had Dad."

"Ah... your dad." She smiled. "Yes, he's a good man and he loves me. Not that there weren't plenty of other men out there that couldn't have loved me." She made a flourish with her hands to indicate her figure. This made us both laugh. "What makes your dad special is that I love him, too."

I stayed until she asked me if I was going to join them for dinner.

"No. I better go. I've been gone for a long time and I haven't really had the chance to talk with White yet. Maybe he does have a job for me and I just don't know it."

"Knock 'em dead," She said and I knew it wasn't just an expression.

BACK AT THE OFFICE BUILDING I struggled with where to go. I pressed the seventh floor but immediately pushed the twelfth when the doors opened to the floor where White was sure to be.

Inside my apartment, I paced. I wanted to call White. I wanted to find out if what Will said was true. The hurt in his eyes last night made me hope that Will had been right, but that same hurt made it impossible for me to pick up my phone or walk back to the elevator. Instead I continued to pace until someone knocked at my door.

I literally jumped a few extra inches with my next pacing step. *Please be him.* I begged of anyone or anything that might be listening.

When I opened the door Red pushed past me carrying a bag from a nearby Chinese restaurant.

"I brought dinner."

My jaw dropped. Red had never brought me food before. I wondered what he wanted, so I asked.

"I thought we should catch up." He pulled food from the bag and readied the plates and utensils.

I joined him at my kitchen bar.

"Is this doctor-patient?"

"Partly. I need to keep up on your state of mind but I thought dinner could be nice. The bar setting I have upstairs helps loosen the men's tongues, but it's not so good on you."

I couldn't stop my eyes from rolling upward as he dished up our plates.

"Do you want some pepper steak?" He held up a huge spoonful of food.

"Sure." I took a seat in front of the plate he'd already covered with rice.

He always seemed to have an ulterior motive. I wondered what it was this time. His most recent behavior had me on edge, and though I remembered a brief time in which we actually got along, I wasn't ready to just let him back in with open arms.

We ate in silence for at least five minutes before he asked how I felt about my recent EOD training.

I told him it had probably been my least favorite activity since joining White and Associates.

"Why's that?"

"It's the possibility of blowing up with my project that I don't like."

"I thought you would've liked having the power."

"It can be empowering, but it's too nerve-racking. I can take all the precautions and still not have full control. Most accidents in this line of work, if the person is careful and diligent, are caused by outside influences beyond our knowledge or power."

"So it makes you feel out of control?"

This type of question coming from Red always put me on edge. I hate being judged.

"I guess."

"That's the same reason I don't care for EOD."

His admission took a little of the edge off.

Did he want me to add something after his admission? There was no way I was going to.

We ate in silence for a few minutes more before his questions began again.

"Going back a little. I'd like to hear about the training op you and Black did in Wyoming. Did you enjoy it?"

"I guess it was fun."

"How about flight training? What did you think of that?"

"Flight training and flying are probably my favorite things I've done since I joined up." My attitude lifted some with the change of topic.

"Does that have anything to do with your instructor?"

He never failed to piss me off, but I held my composure.

"Do you mean Brown or Malone? Because I've developed a fondness for both of them."

"Do you care more for one or the other?"

"What does this have to do with my job here?"

"Actually." He looked me straight in the face. "A lot."

"And why's that?"

"You work with both Brown and Will and an unprofessional relationship could result in problems."

"Do you have problems working with Lacewell?" I asked. Special Agent Lacewell worked for the NSA and we sometimes did jobs for or with her. I'd noticed Red had a soft spot for her.

"What?"

"Do you?"

"Of course not."

"Then consider *that* my answer. Moving along." I slid my plate away.

"Alex, I'm just trying to get a handle on things. If any of us are involved in a relationship outside the company I keep tabs to make sure it doesn't affect our work."

"I suppose that's a tiring job. Keeping track of so many men's sex lives, especially with men like Brown and White." I only meant White, but I added Brown's name in there to throw him off a bit.

"Brown is a bit of a challenge but White hasn't been active on the scene since you joined the company. He's part of the reason I asked about Will."

"You didn't ask about Will," I argued. "You asked about my flight training instructor. You don't talk to me, Red. You talk about me or at me. If you want to know something it would be a lot more respectful to just ask." Even though I thought I did a good job of turning it all back on Red, my thoughts centered on White.

"Fine. I'll spell it out." He pushed his own plate away.

"White hasn't come straight out and told me that he has feelings for you but it's obvious by his lack of interest in other women since you came along. That being noticed and now said, I worry that if you start a relationship with his little brother it could spell trouble for all of us."

"To get you off my ass I'll le you know I have no intentions of starting a relationship with Will, other than one of friendship, and Will is also aware of this. If White has a problem with me becoming friends with his little brother then I'd say he's the only one with problems. That means you're speaking with the wrong person. And, for your information, White hasn't come to see me since I've been back. Hell, he hasn't even called me."

I stood and moved to the other side of the bar and repacked his food into his bag. He didn't take the hint and went back to eating so I dropped my uneaten food into the trash with emphasis. Some of the rice flew back up and landed on my shirt. I wiped it away.

Figures. I'm trying to make a point and I just made a fool of myself.

"The job you have doesn't lend itself well to a long term relationship. You know that, right? All that time away and not being able to talk about what you really do with *anyone.* It's not good for your mental state. I'm surprised you've lasted this long."

"I have plenty of people to talk to. You just aren't one of them and that really bothers you, doesn't it?" Red wore an amused expression so I turned away from him, grabbed my keys and told him to clean up and lock up when he was finished.

I took the stairs to the roof where I spent an hour watching the traffic below.

The door to the roof groaned open. "Red. Leave me the hell alone," I said without turning around.

"It's not Red."

"White." I turned sharply.

"Red told me he pissed you off again because he'd asked about your relationship with Will." He'd walked over to me and stood looking out at the traffic.

"What else did he tell you?" I asked.

"Not much. Did you tell him about us?" He gave me a level look.

"No. You don't have to worry about me telling anyone about *that*. " Tears welled up and I bit my lip to stop them.

"You told Will something." I felt his eyes boring into me.

I'd hoped Will would have kept my confession of love a secret, but they were brothers. What did I expect?

"I said that because Will practically asked me to marry him and I panicked." A single tear escaped and I moved as fast as I could to wipe it away. "He said he wouldn't say anything."

"He asked you to marry him?" White stopped abruptly.

"He didn't get down on one knee or anything. He just said that he had a life plan mapped out and I could fit into that plan. Then he started talking about getting married and having kids. I just blurted it out."

"He didn't tell me exactly what you said. He just said you had plenty to say."

"Oh. I didn't tell him we'd actually—you know."

"What did you say?"

The Chinese food Red had tricked me into eating threatened to reappear. "Nothing really."

He reached over and took my hands in his and turned me toward him. "If you can tell Will, why can't you tell me?"

I fidgeted. There was a piece of rice still on my shoe. My hands were cold and I felt White's warmth on them.

"Why should I tell you?" I pulled my hands away. "You couldn't even call me after I got back."

"Will went up to see you as soon as he was done in my office and then I saw the two of you leave together. How was I supposed to call you?"

"You knew I'd left with Will?"

"Of course I did." He reached up and picked a piece of rice from my hair. "And I knew Will's intentions."

"Why didn't you call me when I was in training?" My voice wavered.

"I did. Brown said you didn't need any more distractions because you were struggling with EOD."

"You called?"

"Yes." Again, he reached for my hands.

My arms were heavy but I lifted my hands to meet White's. As soon as I was in his grip I held on tight. "I missed you." I looked into his eyes.

He pulled me in for a long, deep kiss and then held me close. "I missed you, too."

We stood in each other's arms for a long time before we parted.

"Red knows." White said.

"Did he tell you he knows?"

"No. But, he's been distant and quite pleased with himself since I shipped you off for EOD. He knows something and from the questions he's been asking, it has to be about us."

"Maybe we should just tell the guys."

In some ways I was more than ready to try this in public. It would be a relief and I knew it would boost my confidence in White's feelings and future intentions. Yet, I didn't know if I was ready to answer any questions or deal with the possible consequences.

"Maybe. Red's actually called a meeting in—" he glanced at his watch, "ten minutes. I need you there. I think he's going to tell everyone that you and I are a couple."

"Part of me wants to tell, but the other part worries." I admitted to him.

"I want nothing more than to tell every single man on this planet that you belong to me. But, I don't want to have to defend our relationship."

We stood silent for a few minutes more before White said, "Red wants me to send you off for isolation training next."

I stepped back from the embrace. "How long will that take?"

"Probably at least a month."

"What do *you* think?" I clenched my fists. I'd wait to hear White's opinion before I told him mine. But, if he agreed with Red one more time I'd end this right now. White might find himself trying to learn to fly as he fell from the roof.

"I think you've been gone too much lately. But, if you want to do this, I'll understand."

I let out a shaky breath. "I'd like to hang out here for a while."

"Good. I think Red's just trying to keep us apart. You will have to do the training at some point, though."

"That's fine. I just don't want to take off tomorrow or any time this week." I took a breath. "What're we going to tell the guys if Red brings up our relationship?"

"We're going to admit it and start going out on dates. I wanted to be more confident in this before we told our partners, but it seems like we'll get no privacy now." He gently touched my face. "It'll make our time apart easier if—" he smiled his wicked smile, "if I can actually mark my territory."

I laughed. "We need to invest in a Sharpie marker. I can write my name on the bottom of your foot and you can write yours on mine."

"The thing is, you'll never be *mine.* I could never hope to contain you. You are so much more than meets the eye and could never be domesticated. All I can hope for is to be by your side when you decide what you're going to do next."

Again, I laughed. "I've been yours since I was twelve."

"Twelve?" His brow furrowed and he cocked his head to the side.

"The first time I ever saw you." I looked at the ground in embarrassment.

"When you were twelve?"

"Yes. You came to my house to talk with my dad, remember?"

"I remember that. That's how old you were? Man, I feel old."

We stood in silence for less than a minute before he checked his watch again. "It's almost show time. You ready?"

"I guess. The clandestine meetings were fun while they lasted, at least."

"No. They weren't."

"What?" My stomach hit the floor. Had I really been that bad?

"I can't stand the way other men look at you. Like— like you're available and they might have a chance. I really need to get it out there. Watching you leave with Will yesterday just about killed me. I hadn't even gotten the chance to talk to you were gone again. This will be better. I won't have to make excuses anymore. I can just do what I want to."

"What if Red's *meeting* is about something else?" I still held out hope we could do this on our terms instead of Red's.

"Are you serious about us?" His voice held a slight quiver.

"Yes. You?" As soon as I asked I was terrified of the answer.

"Serious and ready. Lets go get this over with. We can deal with the fallout together."

Chapter Sixteen

ALL OF OUR PARTNERS WERE already in White's office when we arrived. Their quiet conversation stopped as we stepped into the office and all eyes fell on me.

So, this is the way it was going to be. They weren't going to adjust and accept things, there would be blame. And, I was the one to blame.

Red had set up the office as if it were some kind of interrogation. White and I sat in the only two available chairs that faced the half circle of men.

"Thanks for coming, everyone. As I said, I have information about Ms. Grey that I think you all should know."

What? Information about *me* , not White and Grey? What the hell was he up to? I looked at White and his expression was of complete confusion.

White said, "What are you talking about? You didn't tell me anything of the sort."

"Hold on, White. I'm sure you'll be interested in this information. I didn't tell you any more about this meeting than I did because I didn't want you to hide her away." Red narrowed his eyes at me.

"What the hell are you talking about?"

"We all know you and Grey have a thing going on. It's obvious and it's okay. Just let me show you what you should know." He walked to Green and took a manila envelope from him and passed it off to Black. Black looked quizzically at me before he opened the envelope and pulled out photographs.

White reached over and took my hand in his and leaned into me. "Penumbra," he whispered in my ear. I breathed hard and nodded. I hoped we were wrong.

He stood from the chair and ripped the photos away from Black and flipped through them.

"Red." He shook his head ominously. "You shouldn't have done this."

"I wondered if you knew. I'm disappointed in you, White. How could you keep this from us?" Red waved his hands around.

Black stood. "What's this about? All I saw were some surveillance pictures of Grey. Who did you have following her?"

"I did it." Green stood. "I watched her do it." He wore a broad grin. "I don't feel the same way as Red. This isn't a bad thing. I think we can use this is an advantage." He gave me an encouraging nod.

I lifted my chin. I had at least two of my partners in my corner.

"I'm confused," Brown said.

"Let them look at the pictures, White." Red reached for them.

"No." White handed me the pictures and I glanced through them. There were pictures of me sitting on the bench in Brazil as well as pictures of my fight with Flores."

I stood and tossed the pictures to the floor. They spread out for everyone to see. "Some good action shots, Green. Thanks." I gave him a nod back and not one of encouragement.

"Seems like Red's going to beat around the bush so—"

"No." White turned to me.

"It's okay. Red *will* tell them. Look at him. He's rabid with his secret. He can't keep it."

"Grey?" Blue's voice had taken on a sickly air. "What did you do?"

"I took on an additional job title," I said. "It's my legacy. It's what I've been trained for since birth. It's what my parents gave me. My mother, in particular."

"Your mother?" Black asked.

I nodded.

Red smirked. "Come on, Grey. Get to it already. I've been waiting for you to admit something, anything, since you came to us."

Blue had picked up the pictures and finished flipping through them before he handed them to Black.

"For real?" He asked. "Are you really?"

Since Red took terrible offense to my extra title I assumed all of the men would be just as upset. Green's instant acceptance had given me hope and so did Blue's enthusiasm.

"They kept this from all of us. How can you be happy about this?" Red raised his voice.

"I agree with Green. This is a definite advantage for us."

Black tossed the pictures back to the floor. "Penumbra?"

"What?" Brown blurted, grabbing for the photos.

Black shook his head in disgust. "Why didn't you tell me?" He'd made his way across the room. I instinctively cringed but didn't resist when he grabbed my arms in an almost crushing grip. He lifted me from the ground making me make eye contact. Being held up by my arms hurt, but I felt like I deserved it. I had let him down and I understood the pain I saw in his eyes. I would never complain about the bruises I was sure to have.

"Black." I was still breathing heavily. "I couldn't."

"Let her go, Black." White had assumed a fighting position.

Black glanced at White and laughed. "You'd never win, White." But he set me down anyway.

"I suppose you couldn't. I'm sorry I didn't have any idea." Black's expression had faded from one of anger to one of acceptance. Yet, his face didn't show any of the enthusiasm that Blue's had.

"Penumbra?" Brown was still flipping through the pictures. "This was your mugging and your extra long stay in a tanning bed?"

I nodded.

"When's your next job?" Blue asked.

"There will be no more," I answered him. I felt a huge loss. "Thank you for relieving me of this burden, Red." I turned to leave.

"Alex, wait." White grabbed my arm. "What are you doing?"

I winced from the pain. "I can't do this anymore. I didn't like hiding, but it was better than the alternative." All of my energy gone, I barely got the words out.

This was the worst thing that could have happened. I knew I'd been groomed to be Penumbra, but what I didn't realize, until it was time to give her up, was that I *was* Penumbra.

"You can't leave." Black said in a matter-of-fact tone.

"I have to."

"We're big boys," Brown added. "We'll keep our mouths shut."

"Not all of you, obviously." I gave Red and Green a look and the rest of my partners followed my gaze. "Look at it this way. If Red and Green can figure this out, so can anyone

else. That puts everyone I know in danger. I'm done."

"Not necessarily," White said. "This could be better.

Now you have more than just me and Colin to watch your

back." His look pleaded with me.

I was tired. "No." I walked out of the office with them all

talking to me at once.

Chapter Seventeen

I PACKED A BAG AS QUICKLY as I could and got right back onto the elevator, bound for the lobby. I hoped my partners would take a long time in White's office discussing this news. It was probably the juiciest dirt they'd ever had on anyone.

My luck held and I made it to my car without seeing anyone but the lobby guard.

I drove around for an hour before I pulled into a city park for a break. My mind hadn't settled. I couldn't think straight. How was I going to tell my parents and Colin? I'd screwed up. I'd not been careful enough. All their hard work and preparation was for nothing. I'd wasted their time. I put my head in my hands and leaned against the steering wheel.

I remained in that position until my cell phone rang. I dug it out of my back pocket. It was White.

"Red left. Why don't you come down and talk with the rest of us about this."

"No. You can answer all their questions. I'll call you later." I hung up before he could protest.

I sat in the park until long after the sun rose. The call from White had helped clear my head a little. I'd calmed down enough to go back over the plans I'd made if this ever happened.

Since I'd taken on the title I had spent many hours planning what I would and should do if my partners found out who I really was. Now it was time to refine my plan, according to the specifics of the scenario, and carry it out.

I turned the engine over and drove directly to my bank. I took out enough cash to get me through a year, if need be. I still didn't know exactly which plan I'd follow, but having large amounts of cash on me was the first step in every instance.

I drove away from the city for the rest of the day. After the sun started to set I found a small town and rented a room in a tiny motel.

My phone rang every hour or so. Shortly after five o'clock it rang every half an hour. It was time to call White back. I decided I'd get comfortable in my room, get something to eat and then give him a call. The drive away from White and Associates had done a lot to calm my nerves. I'd been able to think through what had really happened back there.

Most of my partners would support me through this, but I needed all of them. Red was my enemy now and enemies of Penumbra turned up dead. It would be okay if they turned up dead at the hands of Penumbra. I could control that. But, they didn't, not always. Other factions made that decision, my father to be specific. I hoped White had been smart enough not to call the Admiral and give him the story yet.

I took out my cell phone and called Colin.

"Colin?"

"Alex? What's wrong?"

"I didn't know if I'd catch you at home. I'm glad I did," I said.

"What's wrong?" He must have been able to hear my deep sorrow.

"I had a falling out with Red and I left the city. I just wanted to let you know that I won't be around for a while. And ask some favors."

"What the hell happened?" His tone had me picturing him red faced and clenching his fists.

"It doesn't matter. Not a big deal, really. I've just had enough of him."

"Where are you? I'll come and get you."

"No. Thanks. I left the city and I'm going to be gone for a while. I'm going off the grid, but I'll be in touch. I promise.

I'm going to need you to set up jobs for me at some point, if you would."

"You mean—" The lilt in his voice let me know the unspoken word was Penumbra.

"Yes. And others, if you have them."

"What about White? That's his job."

"I know. I'm not having troubles with White, but I don't want any contact with the company for a while. I don't know when I'm going back and I don't want to have to explain myself anymore."

"What the hell did Red do?"

I shook my head. "It really isn't a big deal. Actually, it's a whole lot of little things that just built up until he really pissed me off. I need time, but I don't want to just sit around. Might as well be making money while I'm gone."

"Do you need anything?" He asked after several seconds of silence.

"No. I'm good. I'll be getting rid of this phone, though. I don't want the guys tracking me. So, if you get a call from an unrecognizable number, answer it, okay?"

"Okay. Give me a call next week. I'm sure I can have a job for you by then."

"Thanks, Colin. Oh. Could you please tell my dad that I'm okay and that I promise to keep in touch with you? I don't want him or mom to worry too much."

"Of course. Take care of yourself, Alex. Talk to you next week."

I TOOK A DEEP BREATH and dialed White.

"Alex?" White sounded panicked.

"Hey," I said.

"Where are you?"

"I left. Did you call the Admiral yet?"

"Not yet."

"Don't."

"Why? Don't you think he should know?"

"Maybe. But, if you don't want Red to disappear, don't call."

The other end of the line was quiet for some time.

I finally said, "I need some time to work through this and I couldn't do it there. Not with everyone and their questions and accusations."

"I understand. I won't call the Admiral."

"I'll be in touch. I promise. Just not again from this phone. I can't have Red tracking me down again."

I hung up the phone before he could answer.

I might not care for Red, but he really was one of the good guys. He didn't deserve to die or be held against his will because he didn't trust me. He'd had good reason not to trust me. I'd been hiding something. He was protecting his partners and the company. What he did was understandable. I just wished he'd talked to me about it before he brought it up in a meeting. I tried to give him the tools to be my friend. He wouldn't talk to me. He'd been seeing me as his enemy from the very beginning. If he'd have shown me his proof

privately the conversation might have had a much better

ending. For all of us.

My sobs became uncontrollable. I curled up on my bed.

I might never see White again. I knew that. I wondered if he

did. The only way to handle this, and protect Red was to lose

Ms. Grey, not Penumbra.

THE END

-oOo-

Discover other titles by <u>J.C. Phelps</u> at
Amazon.com

The Alexis Stanton Chronicles

<u>Color Me Grey</u>
<u>Shades of Grey</u>
<u>Reflections of Grey</u>
<u>Traces of Grey</u>
<u>Fragments of Grey</u>
<u>Edge of Grey</u>

About the author

J.C. Phelps is a wife and mother of three who writes from the beautiful Black Hills of South Dakota. Somehow, in the middle of the chaos of caring for her daughters, a growing collection of chickens, ducks, and geese, and tending a large garden, she finds the time to write. The Alexis Stanton Chronicles have been the most enjoyable works she's written. Color Me Grey, the first book in the series, introduces the characters she has come to love.

Connect with the author online

Facebook J.C. Phelps
Email authorjcphelps@yahoo.com
Blog http://jcphelps.blogspot.com
Website www.msgrey.com